ULCERVILLE

The ulcer-ridden nabobs of Madison Avenue
had a little problem of . . .

MURDER

They'd just completed running a million-dollar
contest. The only man who knew all the answers
had just been murdered. Five angry contestants
were already claiming the dough.

SCANDAL

If the public ever found out, there'd be a
nationwide scandal. The big boys were all
shaking in their handmade shoes.

A CASE FOR NERO WOLFE

AND FOUR TO GO

BEFORE MIDNIGHT

CHAMPAGNE FOR ONE

CURTAINS FOR THREE

THE FATHER HUNT

THE FINAL DEDUCTION

IN THE BEST FAMILIES

MIGHT AS WELL BE DEAD

MURDER BY THE BOOK

PRISONER'S BASE

THE SECOND CONFESSION

THREE DOORS TO DEATH

THREE FOR THE CHAIR

THREE MEN OUT

THREE WITNESSES

TROUBLE IN TRIPLICATE

A NERO WOLFE MYSTERY

BEFORE
MIDNIGHT
REX STOUT

BANTAM BOOKS
TORONTO • NEW YORK • LONDON • SYDNEY

This low-priced Bantam Book
has been completely reset in a type face
designed for easy reading, and was printed
from new plates. It contains the complete
text of the original hard-cover edition.
NOT ONE WORD HAS BEEN OMITTED.

BEFORE MIDNIGHT

A Bantam Book / published by arrangement with
The Viking Press

PRINTING HISTORY

Viking edition published October 1955
Dollar Mystery Guild edition published January 1956
Serialization in OMNIBOOK June 1956

Bantam edition / July 1957

2nd printing .... August 1957	7th printing .... May 1971
3rd printing .... July 1963	8th printing .... March 1972
4th printing .... July 1963	9th printing . November 1972
5th printing .... August 1965	10th printing . November 1976
6th printing .... May 1971	11th printing ...... August 1981

ISBN 0-553-14797-8

Published simultaneously in the United States and Canada

Bantam Books are published by Bantam Books, Inc. Its trade-
mark, consisting of the words "Bantam Books" and the por-
trayal of a bantam, is Registered in U.S. Patent and Trademark
Office and in other countries. Marca Registrada. Bantam
Books, Inc., 666 Fifth Avenue, New York, New York 10103.

PRINTED IN THE UNITED STATES OF AMERICA

20 19 18 17 16 15 14 13 12 11

Before Midnight

1

Not that our small talk that Tuesday evening in April had any important bearing on the matter, but it will do for an overture, and it will help to explain a couple of reactions Nero Wolfe had later. After a dinner that was featured by one of Fritz's best dishes, squabs with sausage and sauerkraut, in the dining room of the old brownstone house on West Thirty-fifth Street, I followed Wolfe across the hall to the office, and, as he got some magazines from the table near the big globe and went to his chair behind his desk, asked if there were any chores. That was insurance. I had notified him that I intended to take Thursday afternoon off for the opening of the baseball season at the Polo Grounds, and when Thursday came I didn't want any beefing about my letting things pile up.

He said no, no chores, got all his vast bulk adjusted in the chair, the only chair on earth he approved of, and opened a magazine. He allotted around twenty minutes a week for looking at advertisements. I went to my desk, sat, and reached for the phone, then changed my mind, deciding a little more insurance wouldn't hurt. Swiveling and seeing that he was scowling at the open magazine, I got up and circled around near enough to see what he was focused on. It was a full-page ad, black and white, that I and many millions of my fellow citizens knew by heart—though it didn't require much study, since there were only six words in it, not counting repetitions. At the center near the top was a distinguished-looking small bottle, labeled in fancy script *Pour Amour,* with the *Amour* beneath the *Pour.* Right below it were two more of the same, also centered, and below them three more, and then four more, and so on down the page. At the bottom seven bottles stretched clear across, making the base of a twenty-eight-bottle pyramid. In the space at the top left was the statement:

Pour Amour

means

For Love

and at top right it said:

Pour Amour

is

for love

"There are two things about that ad," I said.

Wolfe grunted and turned a page.

"One thing," I said, "is the name itself. To sixty-four and seven-tenths per cent of the women seeing it, it will suggest 'paramour,' and the percentage would be higher if more of them knew what a paramour is. I won't decry American womanhood. Some of my best friends are women. Very few of them want to be or have paramours, so you couldn't come right out and name a perfume that. Put it this way. They see the ad, and they think, So they have the nerve to suggest their snazzy old perfume will get me a paramour! I'll show 'em! What do they think I am? Half an ounce, ten bucks. The other thing—"

"One's enough," he growled.

"Yes, sir. The second thing, so many bottles. That's against the rules. The big idea in a perfume ad is to show only one bottle, to give the impression that it's a scarce article and you'd better hurry up and get yours. Not Pour Amour. They say, Come on, we've got plenty and it's a free country and every woman has a right to a paramour, and if you don't want one prove it. It's an entirely new approach, one hundred per cent American, and it seems to be paying off, it and the contest together."

I had expected to get the desired results by that time, but all he did was sit and turn pages. I took a breath.

"The contest, as you probably know since you look at

2

ads some, is a pip. A million dollars in cash prizes. Each week for nearly five months they have furnished a description of a woman—I might as well give you the exact specifications, since you've been training my memory for years —'a woman recorded in non-fictional history in any of its forms, including biography, as having used cosmetics.' Twenty of them in twenty weeks. This was the description of Number One:

> "Though Caesar fought to give me power
> And I had Antony in my grasp,
> My bosom, in the fatal hour,
> Welcomed the fatal asp.

"Of course that was pie. Cleopatra. Number Two was just as easy:

> "Married to one named Aragon,
> I listened to Columbus' tales,
> And offered all my gems to pawn
> To buy him ships and sails.

"I didn't remember ever reading that Queen Isabella used cosmetics, but since nobody ever bathed in the fifteenth century she must have. I could also give you Numbers Three, Four, and Five, but after that they began to get tough, and by Number Ten I wasn't even bothering to read them. God knows what they were like by the time they got to Twenty—to give you an example, here's Number Seven or Eight, I forget which:

> "My eldest son became a peer
> Although I couldn't write my name;
> As Mr. Brown's son's fondest dear
> I earned enduring fame.

"I call that fudging. Considering how many Mr. Browns have had sons in the course of history, and how many of the sons—"

"Pah." Wolfe turned a page. "Nell Gwynn, the English actress."

I stared. "Yeah, I've heard of her. How come? One of her boy friends may have been named Brown or Brown-

3

son, but that wasn't what made her famous. It was some king."

"Charles the Second." He was smug. "He made his son by her a duke. His father, Charles the First, on a trip to Spain in his youth, had assumed the name of Mr. Brown. And of course Nell Gwynn was the mistress of Charles the Second."

"I prefer paramour. Okay, so you've read ten thousand books. What about this one—I think it was Number Nine:

> *"By the law himself had earlier made*
> *I could not be his legal wife;*
> *The law he properly obeyed*
> *And loved me all my life."*

I flipped a hand. "Name her."

"Archie." His head turned to me. "You have somewhere to go?"

"No, sir, not tonight. Lily Rowan has a table at the Flamingo Room and thought I might drop in for a dance, but I told her you might need me, and she knows how indispensable I—"

"Pfui." He started to glare and decided it wasn't worth the trouble. "You intended to go, and undertook to shift the responsibility for your absence by pestering me into suggesting it. You have succeeded. I suggest that you go somewhere at once."

There were three or four things I could have said, but he sighed and went back to the magazine, so I skipped it. As I headed for the hall his voice told my back, "You shaved and changed your clothes before dinner."

That's the trouble with working for and living with a really great detective.

2

Since I got home late that night and there was nothing urgent on, it was after nine Wednesday morning before I got down to the kitchen for my snack of grapefruit,

4

oatmeal, griddle cakes, bacon, blackberry jam, and coffee. Wolfe had of course breakfasted in his room as usual and gone up to the plant rooms on the roof for his morning session with the orchids.

"It is a good thing, Archie," Fritz remarked, spooning batter, his own batter, onto the griddle for my fourth cake, "to see you break your fast with proper leisure. Disturbed by no interruptions."

I finished a paragraph in the *Times* on the rack before me, swallowed, sipped some coffee, and spoke. "Fritz, I'll be honest with you. There's no one else on earth I could stand in the same room while I'm eating breakfast and reading the morning paper. When you speak you leave it entirely up to me whether I reply, or even whether I listen. However, you should know that I understand you. Take what you just said. What you meant was that no interruptions means no clients and no cases, and you're wondering if the bank account is getting too low for comfort. Right?"

"Yes." He flipped the thick golden-brown disc onto my plate. "But if you think I am worried, no. It is never a question of worry here. With Mr. Wolfe and you—"

The phone rang. I took it there on the kitchen extension, and a deep baritone voice told me it was Rudolph Hansen and wanted to speak to Nero Wolfe. I said Mr. Wolfe wouldn't be available until eleven o'clock but I would take a message. He said he had to see him immediately and would be there in fifteen minutes. I said nothing doing before eleven unless he told me why it was so urgent. He said he would arrive in fifteen minutes and hung up.

Meanwhile Fritz had ditched the cake because it had been off the griddle too long, and started another one.

Ordinarily when a stranger has made an appointment I do a little research on him in advance, but I wouldn't have got very far in a quarter of an hour, and anyway I had another cake and cup of coffee coming. I had just finished and gone to the office with the *Times* to put it on my desk when the doorbell rang. When I went to the hall I saw out on the stoop, through the one-way glass panel in the door, not one stranger but four—three middle-aged men and one who had been, all well dressed and two with homburgs.

I opened the door the two inches that the chain bolt allowed and spoke through the crack. "Your names, please?"

"I'm Rudolph Hansen. I telephoned."

"And the others?"

"This is ridiculous! Open the door!"

"It only seems ridiculous, Mr. Hansen. There are at least a hundred people within a hundred miles, which takes in Sing Sing, who would like to tell Mr. Wolfe what they think of him and maybe prove it. I admit you're not hoods, but with four of you—names, please?"

"I'm an attorney-at-law. These are clients of mine. Mr. Oliver Buff. Mr. Patrick O'Garro. Mr. Vernon Assa."

The names were certainly no help, but I had had time to size them up, and if I knew anything at all about faces they had come not to make trouble but to get out from under some. So I opened the door, helped them put their hats and coats on the big old walnut rack, ushered them into the office and onto chairs, sat at my desk, and told them:

"I'm sorry, gentlemen, but that's the way it is. Mr. Wolfe never comes to the office until eleven. The rule has been broken, but it takes a lot of breaking. The only way would be for you to tell me all about it and persuade me to tackle him, and then for me to go and tell him all about it and try to persuade him. Even if I succeeded, all that would take twenty-five minutes, and it's now twenty-five to eleven, so you might as well relax."

"Your name's Goodwin," Hansen stated. His baritone didn't sound as deep as it had on the phone. I had awarded him the red leather chair near the end of Wolfe's desk, but, with his long thin neck and gray skin and big ears, he clashed with it. A straight-backed painted job with no upholstery would have suited him better.

"Mr. Goodwin," he said, "this is a confidential matter of imperative urgency. I insist that you tell Mr. Wolfe we must see him at once."

"We all do," one of the clients said in an executive tone. Another had popped up from his chair as soon as he sat down and was pacing the floor. The third was trying to keep a match steady enough to light a cigarette. Seeing that I was in for a pointless wrangle, I said politely,

"Okay, I'll see what I can do," and got up and left the room.

In the kitchen, Fritz, who was cleaning up after breakfast and who would never have presumed to ask in words if it looked like business, asked it with a glance as I entered and went to the table where the phones were. I lifted my brows at him, took the house phone, and buzzed the plant rooms.

In a minute Wolfe growled in my ear. "Well?"

"I'm calling from the kitchen. In the office are four men with Sulka shirts and Firman shoes in a panic. They say they must see you at once."

"Confound it—"

"Yes, sir. I'm merely notifying you that we have company. I told them I'd see what I can do, and that's what I can do." I hung up before he could, took the other phone, and dialed a number.

Nathaniel Parker, the lawyer Wolfe always calls on when he is driven to that extremity, wasn't in, but his clerk, Sol Ehrlich, was, and he had heard of Rudolph Hansen. All he knew was that Hansen was a senior partner in one of the big midtown firms with a fat practice, and that he had quite a reputation as a smooth operator. When I hung up I told Fritz that there was a pretty good prospect of snaring a fee that would pay our wages for several months, provided he would finish waking me up by supplying another cup of coffee.

When the sound came, at eleven o'clock on the dot, of Wolfe's elevator starting down, I went to the hall, met him as he emerged, reported on Hansen, and followed him into the office. As usual, I waited to pronounce names until he had reached his chair behind his desk, because he doesn't like to shake hands with strangers, and then Hansen beat me to it. He arose to put a card on Wolfe's desk and sat down again.

"My card," he said. "I'm Rudolph Hansen, attorney-at-law. These gentlemen are clients of mine—that is, their firm is. Mr. Oliver Buff. Mr. Patrick O'Garro. Mr. Vernon Assa. We've lost some valuable time waiting for you. We must see you privately."

Wolfe was frowning. The first few minutes with prospective clients are always tough for him. Possibly there

7

will be no decent excuse for turning them down, and if not he'll have to go to work. He shook his head. "This is private. You glance at Mr. Goodwin. He may not be indispensable, but he is irremovable."

"We prefer to see you alone."

"Then I'm sorry, sir. You have indeed lost time."

He looked at his clients, and so did I. Oliver Buff, the one who had finished with middle age, had a round red face that made his hair look whiter, and his hair made his face look redder. He and Hansen wore the homburgs. Patrick O'Garro was brown all over—eyes, hair, suit, tie, shoes, and socks. Of course his shirt was white. The eyes were bright, quick, and clever. Vernon Assa was short and a little plump, with fat shoulders, and either he had just got back from a month in Florida or he hadn't needed to go. The brown getup would have gone fine with his skin, but he was in gray with black shoes.

"What the hell," he muttered.

"Go ahead," Buff told Hansen.

The lawyer returned to Wolfe. "Mr. Goodwin is your employee, of course?"

"He is."

"He is present at this conversation in his capacity as your agent?"

"Agent? Very well. Yes."

"Then that's understood. First I would like to suggest that you engage me as your counsel and hand me one dollar as a retaining fee."

I opened my eyes at him. The guy must be cuckoo. For fee shipments that office was strictly a one-way street.

"Not an appealing suggestion," Wolfe said drily. "You have a brief for it?"

"Certainly. As you know, a conversation between a lawyer and his client is a privileged communication and its disclosure may not be compelled. I wish to establish that confidential relationship with you, lawyer and client, and then tell you of certain circumstances which have led these gentlemen to seek your help. Obviously that will be no protection against voluntary disclosure by you, since you may end the relationship at any moment, but you will be able to refuse a disclosure at the demand of any authority without incurring any penalty. They and I will be at your mercy, but your record and reputation give us

8

complete confidence in your integrity and discretion. I suggest that you retain me for a specific function: to advise you on the desirability of taking a case about to be offered to you by the firm of Lippert, Buff and Assa."

"What is that firm?"

"You must have heard of it. The advertising agency."

Wolfe's lips were going left to right and back again. It was his kind of smile. "Very ingenious. I congratulate you. But as you say, you will be at my mercy. I may end the relationship at any moment, with no commitment whatever."

"Just a minute," O'Garro put in, his clever bright brown eyes darting from Wolfe to Hansen. "Must it be like that?"

"It's the only way, Pat," the lawyer told him. "If you hire him, you either trust him or you don't."

"I don't like it . . . but if it's the only way . . ."

"It is. Oliver?"

Buff said yes.

"Vern?"

Assa nodded.

"Then you retain me, Mr. Wolfe? As specified?"

"Yes. —Archie, give Mr. Hansen a dollar."

I got one from my wallet, suppressing a pointed comment which the transaction certainly deserved, crossed to the attorney-at-law, and handed it over.

"I give you this," I told him formally, "as the agent for Mr. Nero Wolfe."

3

"It's a long story," Hansen told Wolfe, "but we'll have to make it as short as possible. These gentlemen have appointments at the District Attorney's office. I speak as your counsel of matters pertinent to the case to be offered you about which you seek my advice. Have you heard of the murder of Louis Dahlmann?"

"No."

"It was on the radio."

"I don't listen to the radio in the morning. Neither does Mr. Goodwin."

"To hell with the radio," Assa snapped. "Get on, Rudolph."

"I am. One of LBA's big accounts—we call Lippert, Buff and Assa LBA—is Heery Products, Incorporated. One of the Heery products is the line of cosmetics that they call Pour Amour. They introduced it some years ago and it was doing fairly well. Last spring a young man on the LBA staff named Louis Dahlmann conceived an idea for promoting it, and he finally succeeded in getting enough approval of the idea to have it submitted to the Heery people, and they decided they liked it, and it was scheduled to start the twenty-seventh of September. It was a prize contest, the biggest in history, with a first prize of five hundred thousand dollars in cash, second prize two hundred and fifty thousand, third prize one hundred thousand, and fifty-seven smaller prizes. I have to explain it to you. Each week for twenty weeks there appeared in newspapers and magazines a four-line verse, from which—"

"I can save you that," Wolfe told him. "I know about it."

"Did you enter?" O'Garro demanded.

"Enter the contest? Good heavens, no."

"Get on," Assa snapped.

Hansen did so. "The deadline was February fourteenth. The answers had to be postmarked before midnight February fourteenth. There were over two million contestants, and Dahlmann had trained three hundred men and women to handle the checking and recording. When they finished they had seventy-two contestants who had identified all twenty of the women correctly. Dahlmann had more verses ready, and on March twenty-eighth he sent five of them to each of the seventy-two contestants, by airmail to those at a distance, and the answers had to be postmarked before midnight April fourth. It came out a quintuple tie. Five of them correctly identified the five new ones, and Dahlmann telephoned them and arranged for them to come to New York. They would land the first three prizes, the big three, and also two of the ten-thousand-dollar prizes. They came, and last evening he

10

had them to dinner in a private room at the Churchill. Talbott Heery of Heery Products was there, and so were Vernon Assa and Patrick O'Garro. Dahlmann was going to give them five more verses, with a week to solve them, but a woman who lives in Los Angeles objected that she wanted to work at home and would have to take part of the week getting there, so it was arranged to stagger the deadlines for the postmarks according to how long it would take each one to get home. The meeting ended shortly before eleven o'clock, and they left and separated. Four of them, from out of town, had rooms at the Churchill. One who lives in New York, a young woman named Susan Tescher, presumably went home."

"Get on, damn it," Assa snapped.

"I'm making it as brief as possible, Vern. —Dahlmann also presumably went home. He was a bachelor and lived alone in an apartment on Perry Street. A woman came at seven in the morning to get his breakfast, and when she got there this morning he was on the floor of the living room, dead. He was shot through the heart, from the back, and a cushion from a divan was used to muffle the sound. She ran and got the building superintendent, and the police were notified, and they came and went to work. You may need more facts about the murder when they're available—he was found only four hours ago—but you may not, because that's not what you're needed for. You're needed for something more urgent than murder."

I uncrossed my legs. Something more urgent than murder called for muscles set to go.

Hansen was leaning forward, his palms on his knees. "Here's the crux of it. No one knew the answers in that contest but Louis Dahlmann. He had written all the verses himself—the original twenty, the five to break the first tie, with seventy-two contestants, and the five to break the second tie, with five contestants. Of course the answers for the first twenty had to be known to the crew of checkers and recorders, after the deadline had passed and they started to work, but he himself checked the answers of the seventy-two who were in the first tie. With the third group, the five in the second tie, he guarded the verses themselves almost as strictly as the answers. He typed the verses personally and made only seven copies. One copy was placed in a safe deposit vault, one he kept—

11

I'm not sure where—and the other five were given by him last evening to the five contestants at the meeting."

"He kept it in his wallet," O'Garro said.

Hansen ignored it. "Anyway, the point is not the verses but the answers. I speak of the answers to the last group of five verses—the others don't matter now. Of course it was merely the names of five women, with an explanation of the fitness of the verses for them. There was supposed to be only one copy in existence. It had been typed by Dahlmann on an LBA letterhead, signed by him and initialed by Buff, O'Garro, and Assa, with the answers covered so they couldn't see them, and then put in the safe deposit vault, in a sealed envelope, with five men present. So as I said, no one knew the answers but Dahlmann."

"As far as we know," Oliver Buff put in.

"Certainly," the lawyer agreed. "To our knowledge."

"My God, reach the point," Assa rapped out.

"I am. But at the meeting last evening Dahlmann did an extremely reckless thing. When he—"

"Worse than reckless," Buff declared. "Irresponsible! Criminal!"

"That may be a little strong. But it was certainly ill-advised. When he was ready to hand out the new group of verses he took some envelopes from his inside breast pocket, and other things came with them—other papers and his wallet. He passed the envelopes around, and then —you tell it, Pat, you were there."

O'Garro obliged. "After he gave them the envelopes he started to return the other stuff to his pocket, then he hesitated a moment, smiled around at them, opened the wallet, took a piece of folded paper from it and held it up, and told them he wanted to make—"

"No. Exactly what he said."

"He said, 'I just wanted to make sure I wasn't leaving this here on the table. It's the names of the women who fit the verses I just gave you.' Then he slipped the paper back in the wallet and put it in his pocket."

"Criminal!" Buff blurted.

"How soon after that did the meeting end?"

"Almost immediately. They were so anxious to take a look at the verses we couldn't have held them if we had wanted to, and we didn't."

Hansen leaned to Wolfe. "There it is. When Dahl-

12

mann's body was found he was fully dressed, in the same clothes. Everything was in his pockets, including a roll of bills, several hundred dollars, except one thing. The wallet was gone. We want—Lippert, Buff and Assa want you to find out which one of those five people took it, and today if possible. They're in New York. Four of them were going to take planes this morning, but we stopped them by telling them that the police will have to see them." He glanced at his wrist watch. "We have appointments at the District Attorney's office, but they can wait. What do you need to get started fast?"

"Quite a little." Wolfe sighed. "Am I being engaged by the firm of Lippert, Buff and Assa? Is that correct?"

Hansen turned his head. "Oliver?"

"Yes," Buff said, "that's correct."

"I charge extravagantly. The amount of the fee is left open?"

"Yes."

"To hell with the fee," Assa said, a noble attitude.

"Where," Wolfe asked, "is Mr. Lippert?"

"There is no Lippert. He died ten years ago."

"Then he's through with perfume contests. —You said, Mr. Hansen, that you want me to find out which of those five people took the wallet. I won't undertake it. It's too restricted. What if none of them did?"

"For God's sake." Hansen stared. "Who else?"

"I don't know. From what you have told me I think it highly probably it was one of them, indeed it seems almost conclusive, but I won't be bound like that. At least three others knew that paper was in the wallet: Mr. Heery, Mr. O'Garro, and Mr. Assa."

Assa snorted with impatience. O'Garro said, "You're absolutely right. And from a booth in the Churchill I phoned Hansen and Buff and told them about it. Hansen said nothing could be done. Buff wanted me to see Dahlmann and persuade him to destroy the paper, but I talked him out of it."

"All right," Hansen conceded, "it's immaterial anyway. Put it that the job is to find out who took the wallet and got the paper. Is that satisfactory?"

"It is," Wolfe agreed. "It is understood that I am not engaging to expose the murderer."

"No. I mean it's understood. That's for the police, and

I must make it clear. Nothing has been said to the police about Dahlmann's displaying that paper from his wallet last evening, and nothing is going to be said by any of us, including Mr. Heery. The paper has not been mentioned and will not be. The police will of course question the five contestants, probably they already are, and it might be thought certain that some of them will tell about the paper, but I think it doubtful. —What you said, Pat?"

O'Garro nodded. "I only said, from seeing them last evening, they're not fools. They're anything but fools, and there's half a million dollars at stake, not to mention the other prizes. My guess is none of them will mention it. What do you think, Vern?"

"The same," Assa agreed, "except possibly that old hellcat, the Frazee woman. God knows what she'll say."

"But," Hansen told Wolfe, "even if they do mention it, and the police ask us why we didn't, the answer is that we didn't think it worth mentioning because it was so obvious that Dahlmann was only joking. At least it was obvious to us, and we assumed it was to the others. If the police don't accept that, we shall nevertheless utterly reject the notion that Dahlmann had the answers to those five verses on a paper in his wallet, and the corollary that someone killed him to get it. The police are disposed to be discreet, and they often are, but a thing like that would certainly get out."

He had slid so far forward in the red leather chair that he would certainly slide off. He went on, "You may not fully realize how desperate it is. This contest is the most spectacular promotion of the century. A million in prizes with two million contestants, and the whole country is waiting to see the winner. Naturally we have thought of calling in those verses and preparing five new ones, but that would be risky. It would be an admission that we suspect one of them has secured the answers to those verses by killing Dahlmann, implying an admission that Dahlmann had the answers in his wallet. Any one or all of the five contestants could refuse to surrender the verses on the ground that they had accepted them in good faith, and that would be a frightful mess. If LBA declined to proceed as agreed they could sue and almost certainly collect."

He took a piece of paper from his pocket and unfolded it. "This is a schedule of which each one of them has a copy.

"*Susan Tescher, New York City, before noon April nineteenth.*
"*Carol Wheelock, Richmond, Virginia, before midnight April nineteenth.*
"*Philip Younger, Chicago, Illinois, before midnight April nineteenth.*
"*Harold Rollins, Burlington, Iowa, before midnight April nineteenth.*
"*Gertrude Frazee, Los Angeles, California, before midnight April twentieth.*"

He returned the paper to his pocket and slid back in the chair, which was a relief. "That's the postmark deadline for their answers, staggered as I said. It favors Miss Frazee, who was going to take a plane, but she held out for it. Since they're being held in New York they might agree on an extension, but what if Miss Tescher, who lives here, refused? What if she went ahead and sent in her answers before her deadline? Where would we be?"

Wolfe grunted. "In a pickle."

"We certainly would. There's only one possible way out, to learn who got that paper, today or tomorrow if possible, but absolutely before midnight April twentieth, the last deadline. With proof of that we'll have them licked. We can say to them, One of you—and we name him—stole the answers. That makes it impossible to proceed with those verses. Surrender them or not, as you please, but we're going to give you five new verses and new deadlines, and award the prizes on the basis of your answers to them. They'll have to take it. Under those circumstances they would have no alternative. Would they?"

"No," Wolfe conceded. "But the one exposed as the purloiner of the answers wouldn't have much opportunity for research. He would be jailed on a charge of murder."

"That's his lookout."

"True. Also your guile would be disclosed. The police would know you had lied when you told them that you thought Dahlmann's display of that paper last night was only a joke."

"That can't be helped. Anyway, they'll have the murderer."

"True again. Also," Wolfe persisted, "you're taking an excessive risk in assuming that I will find the thief, with evidence, within a week. I may not. If I don't, you're not in a pickle, you're sunk. Before midnight April Twentieth? I have only this"—he tapped his forehead—"and Mr. Goodwin and a few men I can rely on. Whereas the police have thousands of men and vast resources and connections. I must suggest that you consider taking your problem to them just as you have brought it to me."

"We have considered it. That wouldn't even be risky, it would be certain. By tomorrow morning it would have got out that the answers to the contest had been stolen, and it would be a national scandal, and LBA would have a black eye they might never recover from."

Wolfe was stubborn. "I must be sure you have thought it through. Even if I get the culprit before the deadline it will likewise come out that the answers were stolen."

"Yes, but then we will have the thief, and we'll have arranged to decide the contest in a way agreed to by everybody else concerned. A totally different situation. LBA will be admired and congratulated for dealing with a crisis promptly, boldly, and brilliantly."

"Not by the police."

"No. But by the advertising and business world, the press, and the American people."

"I suppose so." Wolfe's head turned. "I would like to make sure of the decision to dodge with the police. You concur in it, Mr. Buff?"

Buff's big red face had been getting redder, and his brow was moist. "I do," he said. "Because I have to."

"Mr. O'Garro?"

"Yes. We had that out before we came to you."

"Mr. Assa?"

"Yes. You're wasting time!"

"No. If it were a simple matter of catching a murderer —but it isn't. This is full of complexities, and I must know things." Wolfe turned a palm up. "For example. If I were sure that the one who took the wallet actually got the paper with the answers, that would help. But what if he didn't? What if the paper Dahlmann displayed was something else, and it was in fact a hoax, and the thief got nothing for his pains? That would make my job much more difficult and would require a completely different procedure."

"Don't worry," O'Garro assured him. "It was the answers all right. I was there and saw him. Vern?"

"I would say twenty to one," Assa declared. "Louis would get a kick out of showing them the paper with the answers, but just faking it, no. What do you think, Oliver?"

"You know quite well what I think." Buff was grim. "It was strictly in character. At the age of thirty-two Louis Dahlmann was a great creative genius, and in another ten years he would have been a dominant figure in American advertising, another Lasker. That's what we all thought, didn't we? But he had that lunatic streak in him. Of course that paper was the answers; there's not the slightest doubt. After you phoned me last night, Pat, I would have gone down to his place myself, but what was the use? Even if he had destroyed the paper to humor me, after I left he could have sat down and written another one just like it, and he probably would have. But now I wish I had. Right now the future of LBA is in more danger than at any time in the thirty-eight years I've been with it. On account of him! If he were here now, alive, I tell you it would be hard for me to—" He tightened his lips and let the sentence hang.

Wolfe went to the lawyer. "Are you also convinced, Mr. Hansen, that it was no hoax?"

"I am."

"Then I'll proceed on that assumption until it is disproved. I must first see the five contestants, preferably not together, even though time is pressing." He glanced up at the wall clock. "They may already be engaged with the police, but we'll try. One of you will phone and arrange for one of them to be here at twelve-thirty, and arrange also for the others—one at three, one at six, one at—"

"Why six?" Assa demanded. "Good God, you won't need three hours!"

"I hope not. One should be plenty. But from four to six I'll be occupied with other matters, and—"

"There are no other matters! That's preposterous!"

Wolfe eyed him. "Your firm hasn't hired me by the

hour, Mr. Assa. My schedule isn't subject to direction. I work as I work. One of them at three o'clock, one at six, one at seven, and one at eight. You can tell them that their detention in the city has created certain problems in connection with the contest and that you would like them to confer with me as your firm's representative. You will of course not mention the paper Mr. Dahlmann displayed last evening. I'll have dinner at nine o'clock, and any time after ten-thirty you may call on me for a report."

"I'd like to be present at the interviews," Hansen said. "But I can't at twelve-thirty."

"You can't at all, sir. They're going to be ticklish enough as it is, and I may even banish Mr. Goodwin. He will have an errand, by the way. Where is the safe deposit vault in which the answers were placed?"

"The Forty-seventh Street office of the Continental Trust Company."

"One of you will please meet Mr. Goodwin there at two-thirty, take him to the vault, open the envelopes containing the last five verses and the last five answers, and let him copy them and bring the copies to me. Return the originals to the vault."

"Impossible," O'Garro said positively. "Those envelopes must not be opened."

"Nonsense." Wolfe was beginning to get touchy, as usual when he was compelled to start things moving in his skull. "Why not? Those verses and answers are done for. No matter what happens, they can't possibly be the basis for awarding the prizes. They might, if we could get apodictic proof that there was no paper in Dahlmann's wallet containing the answers, but we can't. Can any of you describe any circumstances in which those verses and answers can now be used? Try it."

They exchanged glances. Wolfe waited.

"You're right," Buff admitted for the firm.

"Then it can do no harm for me to have them, provided Mr. Goodwin and I keep them to ourselves, and it may do some good. I have an idea for using them which may be worth developing. Will one of you meet him at two-thirty?"

"Yes," Buff agreed. "Probably two of us. Those envelopes have been untouchable. Mr. Heery will have to know about it. He may want to be present."

"As you please. By the way, since his firm is as deeply concerned as yours, what about him? Does he know you're hiring me? Does he approve your strategy?"

"Completely."

"Then that will do for now. Please use the phone on Mr. Goodwin's desk. Do you want him to get a number for you?"

They didn't, which was the best proof yet of how desperate they were. Since those birds were up around the top, the top numbers in one of the three biggest agencies in the country, with corner rooms at least twenty by twenty and incomes in six figures, it had of course been years since any of them had personally dialed a number in an office. To expect them to would be against all reason. But when I vacated my chair O'Garro came and took it, asked me for the number of the Churchill, and went ahead and dialed it as if it were a natural and normal procedure. I thought, There you are, a man with eyes as clever as that can do anything.

It took a while. After the rest of us had sat and listened for some minutes he finally hung up and told us, "Two of them were out. Rollins was just leaving for an appointment at Homicide West. Miss Frazee will be here at twelve-thirty."

Hansen, on his feet, said, "We must go, we'll be half an hour late. We'll get them later."

But Wolfe kept them for one more thing, information about the five contestants. They only had enough to fill one page of my notebook, which wasn't much to go on. I went to the hall with them to see that nobody took my topcoat by mistake, let them out, and returned to the office. Wolfe was sitting with his eyes closed and his palms flattened on the desk. I went to my desk and wheeled the machine to me and got out paper, to type the meager dope on the suspects. At the sound of footsteps I turned to see Fritz enter with beer on a tray.

"No," I said firmly. "Take it back, Fritz."

"A woman is coming!" Wolfe bellowed.

"That's only an excuse. The real trouble is that you hate a job with a deadline, especially when you stand about one chance in four thousand. I admit that before midnight April twentieth is one hell of an order, but on January nineteenth at three-twenty-seven p.m. you told me that if you ever rang for beer before lunch I should cancel it and disregard your protests, if any. I don't blame you for losing control, since we're almost certainly going to get our noses bumped, but no beer until after lunch. However, we don't want to embarrass Mr. Brenner."

I went and took the tray from Fritz and convoyed it to the kitchen.

4

If I had known what was on the way to him in the shape of Miss Gertrude Frazee of Los Angeles, founder and president of the Women's Nature League, I wouldn't have had the heart to hijack the beer. And if Wolfe had known, he probably would have refused the case and sent LBA and their counselor on their way.

I should try to describe her outfit, but I won't; I will only say she had swiped it from a museum. As for describing her, it's hard to believe. The inside corners of her eyes were trying to touch above a long thin nose, and nearly made it. Only an inch of brow was visible because straggles of gray hair flopped down over the rest. The left half of her mouth slanted up and the right half slanted down, and that made you think her chin was lower on one side than on the other, though maybe it wasn't. She was exactly my height, five feet eleven, and she strode.

She sat halfway back in the red leather chair, with both hands on her bag in her lap and her back straight and stiff. "I fail to see," she told Wolfe, "that the death of that man has any effect on the contest. Murder or not. There was nothing in the rules about anybody dying."

When she spoke her lips wanted to move perpendicular to the slant, but her jaw preferred straight up and down. You might have thought that after so many years, at least sixty, they would have come to an understanding, but nothing doing.

Wolfe was taking her in. "Certainly, madam, the rules did not contemplate sudden and violent death, and made no provision for it. The contest is affected, not by the death itself, but by the action of the police in asking the contestants not to leave the city until further—"

"They didn't ask me! They told me! They said if I left I would be brought back and arrested for murder!"

I shook my head. So she was that kind. No homicide cop and no assistant DA could possibly have said anything of the sort.

"They are sometimes ebullient," Wolfe told her. "Anyhow, I wanted to discuss not only the contest, but also you. After the prizes are awarded there will be great demand for information about the winners, and my clients want to be able to supply it. The enforced delay gives us this opportunity. My assistant, Mr. Goodwin, will take notes. I assume that you have never married, Miss Frazee?"

"I have not. And I won't." Her eyes took in my notebook. "I want to see anything that's going to be printed about me."

"You will. Have you ever won a prize in a contest?"

"I have never entered a contest. I despise contests."

"Indeed. Didn't you enter this one?"

"Of course I did. That's a stupid question."

"No doubt." Wolfe was polite. "But surely that's an interesting paradox—you despise contests, but you entered one. There must have been a compelling motive?"

"I fail to see that my motive is anybody's business, but I certainly am not ashamed of it. Ten years ago I founded the Women's Nature League of America. We have many thousand members, too many to count. What is your opinion of women who smear themselves with grease and soot and paint and stink themselves up with stuff made from black tar and decayed vegetable matter and tumors from male deer?"

"I haven't formulated one, madam."

"Of course you have. You're a male." Her eyes darted to me. "What's yours, young man?"

"It depends," I told her. "The tumor part sounds bad."

21

"It smells bad. It's been used for thirty centuries. Musk. In the Garden of Eden, when Eve's face was dirty what did she do? She washed it with good clean water. What do women do today? They rub it in with grease! Look at their lips and fingernails and toes and eyelashes—and other places. The Women's Nature League is the champion and the friend of the natural woman, and the natural woman was Eve, Eve the way God made her. The only true beauty is natural beauty, and I know, because I was denied that wondrous gift. I am not merely unlovely, I am ugly. The well-favored ones have no right to pollute the beauty of nature. I know!"

Her back had bowed a little, and she straightened it. "That knowledge came to me early, and it has been my staff and my banner all my life. I have always had to work for my bread, but I saved some money, and ten years ago I used some of it to start the League. We have many members, over three thousand, but the dues are small and we are severely limited. Last fall, last September, when I saw the advertisement of the contest, I thought again what I had thought many times before, that it was hopeless because there was too much money against us, millions and millions, and then, sitting there looking at the advertisement, the idea came to me. Why not use *their* money for *us*? I considered it and approved of it. A majority of our members live in or near Los Angeles, and most of them are cultured and educated women. I phoned to some and asked them to phone others, and all of them were enthusiastic about it and wanted to help. I organized it, and you don't have to be beautiful to know how to organize. Within two weeks there were over three hundred of us working at it. We had no serious trouble with any of the original twenty, the twenty that were published—except Number Eighteen, and we finally got that. With the second group, to break the tie, with those we had to get five in less than a week, which was unfair because the verses were all mailed at the same time in New York and it took longer for them to get to me, and they were harder, much harder, but we got them, and I mailed them ten hours before the deadline. We're going to get these too." She tapped her bag, in her lap. "No question about it. No question at all. We're going to get

22

it, no matter how hard they are. Half a million dollars. For the League."

Wolfe was regarding her, trying not to frown and nearly succeeding. "Not necessarily half a million, madam. You have four competitors."

"The first prize," she said confidently. "Half a million." Suddenly she leaned forward. "Do you ever have a flash?"

The frown won. "Of what? Anger? Wit?"

"Just a flash—of what is coming. I had two of them long ago, when I was young, and then never any more until the day I saw the advertisement. It came on me, into me, so swiftly that I only knew it was there—the certainty that we would get their money. Certainty can be a very sweet thing, very beautiful, and that day if filled me from head to foot, and I went to a mirror to see if I could see it. I couldn't, but it was there, so there has never been any question about it. The first prize. Our budget committee is already working on projects, what to do with it."

"Indeed." The frown was there to stay. "The five new verses, those that Mr. Dahlmann gave you last evening—how did you send them to your colleagues? Telephone or telegraph or airmail?"

"Ha," she said. Apparently that was all.

"Because," Wolfe observed matter-of-factly, "you have sent them, naturally, so they could go to work. Haven't you?"

Her back was straight again. "I fail to see that that is anybody's business. There is nothing in the rules about getting assistance. Nothing was said about it last night. This morning I telephoned my vice-president, Mrs. Charles Draper, because I had to, to tell her I couldn't return today and I didn't know when I could. It was a private conversation."

Evidently it was going to stay private. Wolfe dropped it and switched. "Another reason for seeing you, Miss Frazee, was to apologize on behalf of Lippert, Buff and Assa, my clients, for the foolish joke that Mr. Dahlmann indulged in last evening—when he exhibited a paper and said it was the answers to the verses he had just given you. Not only was it witless, it was in bad taste. I tender you the apologies of his associates."

23

"So that's how it is," she said. "I thought it would be something like that, that's why I came, to find out." Her chin went up and her voice hardened. "It won't work. Tell them that. That's all I wanted to know." She stood up. "You think because I'm ugly I haven't got any brains. They'll regret it. I'll see that they regret it."

"Sit down, madam. I don't know what you're talking about."

"Ha. You're supposed to have brains too. They know that one of them went there and killed him and took the paper, and now they're going—"

"Please! Your pronouns. Are you saying that one of my clients took the paper?"

"Of course not. One of the contestants. That would put them in a hole they couldn't get out of unless they could prove which one took it, so they're going to say it was a joke, there was no such paper, and when we send in the answers they'll award the prizes, and they think that will settle it unless the police catch the murderer, and maybe they never will. But it won't work. The murderer will have the right answers, all five of them, and he'll have to explain how he got them, and he won't be able to. These five are going to be very difficult, and nobody can get them by spending a few hours in a library."

"I see. But you could explain how you got them. Your colleagues at home are working on them now. You're going?"

She had headed for the door, but turned. "I'm going back to the hotel for an appointment with a policeman. I use my brains with them too, and I know my rights. I told them I didn't have to go to see them, they could come to see me unless they arrested me, and they don't dare. I wouldn't let them search my room or my belongings. I've told them what I've seen and heard, and that's all I'm going to tell them. They want to know what I thought! They want to know if I thought the paper he showed us really had the answers on it! I fail to see why I should tell them what I thought—but I'll certainly tell you and you can tell your clients . . ."

She came back to the chair and was sitting down, so I held on to my notebook, but as her fanny touched the leather she said abruptly, "No, I have an appointment," got erect, and strode from the room. By the time I got to the rack in the hall she had her coat on, and I had to move to get to the doorknob before her.

When I returned to the office Wolfe was sitting slumped, taking air in through his nose and letting it out through his mouth, audibly. I stuck my hands in my pockets and looked down at him.

"So I told the cops about Dahlmann showing the paper," I said. "That'll help. Twenty minutes to lunch. Beer? I'll make an exception."

He made a face.

"I could probably," I suggested, "get Los Angeles phone information to dig up a Mrs. Charles Draper, and you could ask her how they're making out with the verses."

"Pointless," he growled. "If she killed him and got the answers, she would certainly have made the call and given her friends the verses. She admits she has brains. If I had had the answers I might . . . but no, that would have been premature. You have an appointment at two-thirty."

"Right. Since expenses are on the house it wouldn't cost you anything to get Saul and Fred and Orrie and Johnny and Bill and hang tails on them, but with four of them living at the Churchill it would be a hell of a job—"

"Useless. If anything is to be learned by that kind of routine the police will get it long before we can. They probably—"

The phone rang. I got it at my desk, heard a deep gruff voice that needed filing, an old familiar voice, asked it to hold on, and told Wolfe that Sergeant Purley Stebbins wished to speak to him. He reached for his instrument, and since I am supposed to stay on unless I am told not to, I did so.

"This is Nero Wolfe, Mr. Stebbins. How do you do."

"So-so. I'd like to drop in to see you—say three o'clock?"

"I'm sorry, I'll be engaged."

"Three-thirty?"

"I'll still be engaged."

"Well . . . I guess it can wait until six. Make it six o'clock?"

Purley knew that Wolfe's schedule, four to six up in the

plant rooms, might be changed for an H-bomb, but nothing much short of that.

"I'm sorry, Mr. Stebbins, but I'll have no time today or this evening. Perhaps you can tell me——"

"Sure, I can tell you. Just a little friendly talk, that's all. I want to get your slant on a murder case."

"I have no slant on any murder case."

"No? Then why the hell——" He bit it off. He went on, "Look, I know you and you know me. I'm no fancy dancer. But how about this, at half-past twelve a woman named Gertrude Frazee entered your premises and as far as I know she's still there. And you have no slant on the murder of a man named Louis Dahlmann? Tell it to Goodwin. I'm not trying to get a piece of hide, I just want to come and ask you some questions. Six o'clock?"

"Mr. Stebbins." Wolfe was controlling himself. "I have no commission to investigate the murder of Louis Dahlmann, or any other. On past occasions you and your associates have resented my presumption in undertaking to invesitgate a homicide. You have bullied me and harried me. When I offend again I shall expect you upon me again, but this time I am not invading your territory, so for heaven's sake let me alone."

He hung up and so did I, synchronizing with him. I spoke. "I admit that was neat and a chance not to be passed up, but wait till he tells Cramer."

"I know." He sounded better. "Is the chain bolt on?"

I went to the hall to make sure, and then to the kitchen to tell Fritz we were under siege.

5

I could merely report that I kept my two-thirty appointment and got the verses and answers, and let it go at that, but I think it's about time you had the pleasure of meeting Mr. Talbott Heery. He was quite a surprise to me, I don't know why, unless I had unconsciously decided what a perfume tycoon should look like and he didn't match. Nor did he smell. He was over six feet, broader than me and some ten years older, and his clear smooth skin, stretched tight over the bones, didn't look as if it had ever needed to be shaved. Nor was there any sign of grease or soot or paint. He might have been a member of the Men's Nature League.

Buff and O'Garro were with him, but not Assa. They had to do some explaining to get me admitted to the vault. Buff and Heery and I went to a small room, and soon O'Garro and an attendant came with the box, only about five by three and eighteen inches long, evidently rented for this purpose exclusively. The attendant left, and O'Garro unlocked the box and opened it, and took out some envelopes, six of them. The sealed flaps had gobs of sealing wax. Four of them had been cut open. He asked me, "You want only the last group of five?"

I told him yes, and he handed me the two uncut envelopes. One of them was inscribed, "Verses, second group of five, Pour Amour Contest," and the other, "Answers, second group of five, Pour Amour Contest." As I got out my knife to slit them open O'Garro said, "I don't want to see them," and backed up against the end wall, and the others followed suit. From that distance they couldn't read typing, but they could watch me, and they did. There were pencils and paper pads on the table, but I preferred my pen and notebook, and sat down and used them. The five four-line verses were all on one sheet, and so were the answers—the names of five women, with brief explanations of the references in the verses.

It didn't take long. As I was folding the sheets and returning them to the envelopes, Buff spoke. "Your name is Archie Goodwin?"

"Right."

"Please write on each envelope, 'Opened, and the contents copied, by Archie Goodwin, on April thirteenth, nineteen-fifty-five, in the presence of Talbott Heery, Oliver Buff, and Patrick O'Garro,' and sign it."

I gave it a thought. "I don't like it," I told him. "I don't want to sign anything so closely connected with a million dollars. How about this: I'll write 'Opened, and the contents copied, by Archie Goodwin, on April thirteenth, nineteen-fifty-five, with our consent and in our presence,' and you gentlemen sign it."

They decided that would do, and I wrote, and they signed, and O'Garro returned the envelopes to the box and locked it, and went out with it. Soon he rejoined us, and the four of us went up a broad flight of marble steps and out to the street. On the sidewalk Heery asked where they were bound for, and they said their office, which was around the corner, and he turned to me. "You, Goodwin?"

I told him West Thirty-fifth Street, and he said he was going downtown and would give me a lift. The others went, and he flagged a taxi and we got in, and I told the driver Thirty-fifth and Ninth Avenue. My watch said ten to three, so I should make it by the time the second customer arrived.

As we stopped for a red light at Fifth Avenue, headed west on Forty-seventh Street, Heery said, "I have some spare time and I think I'll stop in for a talk with Nero Wolfe."

"Not right now," I told him. "He's tied up."

"But now is when I have the time."

"Too bad, but it'll have to be later—in fact, much later. He has appointments that run right through until late this evening, to ten-thirty or eleven."

"I want to see him now."

"Sorry. I'll tell him, and he'll be sorry too. If you want to give me your number I'll ring you and tell you when."

He got a wallet from his pocket, fingered in it, and came up with a crisp new twenty. "Here," he said. "I don't need long. Probably ten minutes will do it."

I felt flattered. A finiff would have been at the market, and a sawbuck would have been lavish. "I deeply appreciate it," I said with feeling, "but I'm not the doorman or receptionist. Mr. Wolfe has different men for different functions, and mine is to collect poetry out of safe deposit boxes. That's all I do."

Returning the bill neatly to the wallet, he stated, with no change whatever in tone or manner, "At a better time and place I'll knock your goddam block off." You see why I wanted you to meet him. That ended the conversation. To pass the time as we weaved along with the traffic I thought of three or four things to say, but after all it was his taxi and it had been nice of him to make it a twenty. When the cab stopped at Thirty-fifth Street I

28

only said, "See you at a better time and place," as I got out.

At the corner drugstore I went to the phone booth, dialed our number, got Wolfe, and was told that no company had come. It may have been a minor point, whether Homicide had tails on all five of them or was giving Miss Frazee special attention, but it wouldn't hurt to find out, so I went down the block to Doc Vollmer's place, thirty yards from Wolfe's, and stepped down into the areaway, from where I could see our stoop. My watch said ten past three. I was of course expecting a taxi and wasn't interested in pedestrians, until I happened to send a glance to the east and saw a figure approaching that I could name. I swiveled my head to look west, and saw a female mounting the seven steps to our stoop. So I moved up to the sidewalk into the path of the approaching figure—Art Whipple of Homicide West. He stopped on his heels, opened his mouth, and closed it.

"I won't tell her," I assured him. "Unless you want me to give her a message?"

"Go chin yourself," he suggested.

"At a better time and place. She'll probably be with us nearly an hour. If you want to go to Tony's around the corner I'll give you a ring just before she leaves. Luck."

I went on to our stoop, and as I was mounting the steps the door opened a crack and Fritz's voice came through it. "Your name, please, madam?"

I said okay, and he slipped the bolt and opened up, and I told the visitor to enter. While Fritz attended to the door I offered to take her coat, a brown wool number that would have appreciated a little freshening up, but she said she would keep it and her name was Wheelock.

I ushered her to the office and told Wolfe, "Mrs. James R. Wheelock, of Richmond, Virginia." Then I went and opened the safe, took the four leaves from my notebook that I had written on, put them in the inner compartment, closed that door and twirled the knob of the combination, and closed the outer door. By the time I got to my desk Carol Wheelock was in the red leather chair, with her coat draped over the back.

According to the information she was a housewife, but if so her house was nearly out of wife. She looked as if she hadn't eaten for a week and hadn't slept for a month.

Properly fed and rested for a good long stretch, filled in from her hundred pounds to around a hundred and twenty, she might have been a pleasant sight and a very satisfactory wife for a man who was sold on the wife idea, but it took some imagination to realize it. The only thing was her eyes. They were dark, set in deep, and there was fire back of them.

"I ought to tell you," she said in a low even voice, "that I didn't want to come here, but Mr. O'Garro said it was absolutely necessary. I have decided I shouldn't say anything to anybody. But if you have something to tell me —go ahead."

Wolfe was glowering at her, and I would have liked to tell her that it meant nothing personal, it was only that the sight of a hungry human was painful to him, and the sight of one who must have been hungry for months was intolerable. He spoke. "You understand, Mrs. Wheelock, that I am acting for the firm of Lippert, Buff and Assa, which is handling the contest for Heery Products, Incorporated."

"Yes, Mr. O'Garro told me."

"I do have a little to tell you, but not much. For one item, I have had a talk with one of the contestants, Miss Gertrude Frazee. You may know that she is the founder and president of an organization called the Women's Nature League. She says that some three hundred of its members have helped her in the contest, which is not an infraction of the rules. She does not say that she has telephoned to them the verses that were distributed last evening, and that they are now working on them, but it wouldn't be fanciful to assume that she has and they are. Have you any comment?"

She was staring at him, her mouth working.

"Three hundred," she said.

Wolfe nodded.

"That's cheating. That's—she can't do that. You can't let her get away with it."

"We may be helpless. If she has violated no rule and nothing that was agreed upon last evening, what then? This is one aspect of the grotesque situation created by the murder of Louis Dahlmann."

"I'll see the others." The fire behind her eyes was showing through. "We won't permit it. We'll refuse to go ahead with those verses. We'll insist on new ones when we're allowed to go home."

"That would suit Miss Frazee perfectly. She would send in her answers before the agreed deadline and demand the first prize, and if she didn't get it she could sue and probably collect. You'll have to do better than that if you want to head her off—emulate her, perhaps. Of course you've had help too—your husband, your friends; get them started."

"I've had no help."

She started to tremble, first her hands and then her shoulders, and I thought we were in for it, but she pulled one that I had never expected to see. Women of all ages and shapes and sizes have started to have a fit in that office. Some I have caught in time with a good shot of brandy, some I have stopped with a smack or other physical contact, and some I have had to ride out—with Wolfe gone because he can't stand it. I left my chair and started for her, but she stuck her tongue out at me. So I thought, but that wasn't it. She was only getting the tongue between her teeth and clamping down on it. Its end bulged and curled up and was purple, but she only clamped harder. It wasn't pretty, but it worked. She stopped trembling, opened her fists and closed them and opened them again, and got her shoulders set, rigid. Then she retrieved her tongue. I had a notion to give her a pat before returning to my chair, in recognition of an outstanding performance, but decided that a woman who could stand off a fit like that in ten seconds flat probably didn't care for pats.

"I beg your pardon," she said.

"Brandy," Wolfe told me.

"No," she said, "I'm all right. I couldn't drink brandy. I guess what did it was what you said about help. I haven't had any. The first few weeks weren't bad, but after that they got harder, and later, when they got really hard . . . I don't know how I did it. I said I wasn't going to say anything, but after what you said about Miss Frazee having three hundred women helping her . . . well. I'm thirty-two years old, and I have two children, and my husband is a bookkeeper and makes fifty dollars a week. I was a schoolteacher before I married. I had been going along for years, just taking it, and I saw this contest and decided to win it. I'm going to have a nice home and a car—two cars, one for my husband and one for me—and I'm going to have some clothes, and I'm going to send my husband to school and make him a CPA if he has it in him. That day I saw the contest, I took charge that day. You know what I mean."

"Indeed I do," Wolfe muttered.

"So when they got hard there was no one I could ask for help, and anyway, if I had got help I would have had to share the prize. I didn't do much eating or sleeping the last seven weeks of the main contest, but the worst was when they sent us five to do in a week to break the tie. I didn't go to bed that week, and I was afraid I had one of them wrong, and I didn't get them mailed until just before midnight—I went to the post office and made them let me see them stamp the envelope. After all that, do you think I'm going to let somebody get it by cheating? With three hundred women working at it while we're not allowed to go home?"

After seeing her handle the fit I didn't think she was going to let somebody get anything she had made up her mind to have, with or without cheating.

"It is manifestly unfair," Wolfe conceded, "but I doubt if it can be called cheating, at least in the legal sense. And as for cheating, it's conceivable that someone else had a bolder idea than Miss Frazee and acted upon it. By killing Mr. Dahlmann in order to get the answers."

"I'm not going to say anything about that," she declared. "I've decided not to."

"The police have talked with you, of course."

"Yes. They certainly have. For hours."

"And they asked you what you thought last evening when Mr. Dahlmann displayed a paper and said it contained the answers. What did you tell them?"

"I'm not going to talk about it."

"Did you tell the police that? That you wouldn't talk about it?"

"No. I hadn't decided then. I decided later."

"After consultation with someone?"

She shook her head. "With whom would I consult?"

"I don't know. A lawyer. A phone call to your husband."

"I haven't got a lawyer. I wouldn't call my husband—I know what he'd say. He thinks I'm crazy. I couldn't pay a lawyer anyway because I haven't got any money. They paid for the trip here, and the hotel, but nothing for incidentals. I was late for my appointment with you because I got on the wrong bus. I haven't consulted anybody. I made the decision myself."

"So you told the police what you thought when Mr. Dahlmann displayed the paper?"

"Yes."

"Then why not tell me? I assure you, madam, that I have only one interest in the matter, on behalf of my clients, to make sure that the prizes are fairly and honestly awarded. You see, of course, that that will be extremely difficult if in fact one of the contestants took that paper from Mr. Dahlmann and it contains the answers. You see that."

"Yes."

"However, it is the belief of my clients—and their contention—that the paper did not contain the answers, that Mr. Dahlmann was only jesting; and that therefore the secrecy of the answers is still intact. Do you challenge that contention?"

"No."

"You accept it?"

"Yes."

"Then you must have told the police that when Mr. Dahlmann displayed the paper you regarded it as a joke, and the sequel is plain: it would be absurd to suspect you of going to his apartment and killing him to get it. So it is reasonable to suppose that you are not suspected. —Archie, your phone call from the corner. Did you see anyone?"

"Yes, sir. Art Whipple. He was here on the Heller case."

"Tell Mrs. Wheelock about it."

I met her eyes. "I was hanging out up the street when you came, and a Homicide detective was following you. I exchanged a few words with him. If you want to spot him when you leave, he's about my size, drags his feet a little, and is wearing a dark gray suit and a gray snapbrim hat."

"He was following me?"

"Right."

Her eyes left me for Wolfe. "Isn't that what they do?"

But her left hand had started to tremble, and she had to grasp it with the other one and squeeze it. Wolfe shut his eyes, probably expecting some more tongue control. Instead, she arose abruptly and asked, "May I have—a bathroom?"

I told her certainly, and went and opened the door of the one partitioned off in the far corner, to the left of my desk, and she came and passed through, closing the door behind her.

She was in there a good quarter of an hour without making a sound. The partitions, like all the inner walls on the ground floor, are soundproofed, but I have sharp ears and heard nothing whatever. I said something to Wolfe, but he only grunted. After a little he looked up at the clock: twenty to four. Thereafter he looked at it every two minutes; at four sharp he would leave for the plant rooms. There were just nine minutes to go when the door in the partition opened and she was back with us.

She came and stood at Wolfe's desk, across from him. "I beg your pardon," she said in her low even voice. "I had to take some pills. The food at the hotel is quite good, but I simply can't eat. I haven't eaten much for quite a while. Do you want to tell me anything else?"

"Milk toast," Wolfe said gruffly. "My cook, Fritz Brenner, makes it superbly. Sit down."

"I couldn't swallow it. Really."

"Then hot bouillon. Our own. It can be ready in eight minutes. I have to leave you, but Mr. Goodwin—"

"I couldn't. I'm going back to the hotel and see the others about Miss Frazee—I think I am—I'll think about it on the bus. That's cheating." She had moved to get her coat from the back of the chair, and I went and held it for her.

Knowing what bus crowds were at that time of day, and thinking it wouldn't break LBA, I made her take a buck for taxi fare, but had to explain it would go on the expense list before she would take it. When, in the hall, I had let her out and bolted the door and turned, Wolfe was there, opening the door of his elevator.

"You put the answers in the safe," he stated.

"Yes, sir, inner compartment. I told you on the phone that Buff and O'Garro and Talbott Heery were there, but I didn't report that Heery brought me downtown in a taxi

34

so he could offer me twenty bucks to get him in to see you right away. I told him—"

"Verbatim, please."

I gave it to him, which was nothing, considering that he will ask for a whole afternoon's interviews with five or six people verbatim, and get it. At the end I added, "For a footnote, Heery couldn't knock my block off unless he got someone to hold me. Do you want to squeeze him in somewhere?"

He said no, Heery could wait, and entered the elevator and shut the door, and I went to the office. There were a few daily chores which hadn't been attended to, and also my notes of the talks with Miss Frazee and Mrs. Wheelock had to be typed. Not that it seemed to me there was anything in them that would make history. I admitted that Wolfe was only going fishing, hoping to scare up a word or fact that would give him a start, and that he had got some spectacular results from that method more than once before, but in this case genius might have been expected to find a short cut. There were five of them, which would take a lot of time, and the time was strictly rationed. Before midnight April twentieth.

I was in the middle of the Frazee notes when the phone interrupted me, and when I told it, "Nero Wolfe's office, Archie Goodwin speaking," a male voice said, "I want to speak to Mr. Wolfe. This is Patrick O'Garro."

They were certainly popping the precedents. He should have told his secretary, and she should have got me and spent five minutes trying to lobby me into putting Wolfe on. The best explanation was that they were playing it so close to their chins they were even keeping it from the staff that they had hired Nero Wolfe.

"He's engaged," I said, "and if I disengage him for a phone call it would have to be good. Can't you use me for a relay?"

"I want to ask him if he's made any progress."

"If he has it's in his head. He told you he would report later this evening. He has seen Miss Frazee and Mrs. Wheelock. How about the others?"

"That's why I'm calling. Susan Tescher will be there at six, and Harold Rollins at seven, but Younger can't come. He's in bed at the hotel with heart flutters. They sent him up from the District Attorney's office in an ambulance. He wouldn't go to a hospital. My doctor saw him and says it's not serious, but he's staying in bed until the doctor sees him tomorrow."

I said I'd tell Wolfe and got the number of Younger's room. After I hung up I got at the house phone and buzzed the plant rooms, and in a minute Wolfe's voice blurted at me, "Well?"

"O'Garro just phoned. One's coming at six and one at seven, but at the DA's office Philip Younger's heart began to flutter and he's at the hotel in bed. Shall I go up and sit with him?"

"You must be back by six o'clock."

I said I would and the connection went.

There was a slight problem. Years before, after a certain episode, I had made myself promise that I would never go on any errand connected with a murder case without a gun, but this wasn't a murder case by the terms agreed upon. The job was to nail a thief. I decided that was quibbling, got my shoulder holster from the drawer and put it on, got the Marley .32 and loaded it and slipped it into the holster, went to the hall, and called to Fritz to come and bolt the door after me.

6

It was safe to assume that the floor clerk on the eighteenth floor of the Churchill would be stubborn about it, since journalists were certainly stalking the quintet, so I anticipated her by first finding Tim Evarts, the hotel's first assistant security officer, not to be called a house dick, who owed me a little courtesy from past events. He obliged by phoning her, after I promised to set no fires and find no corpses, and all she did was look at both sides of my card and one side of me and wave me on.

Eighteen-twenty-six was about halfway down a long corridor. There was no one in sight anywhere except a chambermaid with towels, and I concluded that the city employees hadn't invaded the hotel itself for surveillance.

My first knock on the door of eighteen-twenty-six got me an invitation to come in, not too audible, and I opened the door and entered, and saw that LBA had done well by their guests. It was the fifteen-dollar size, with the twin beds headed against the wall at the left. On one of them, under the covers, was Old King Cole with a hangover, his mop of white hair tousled and his eyes sick.

I approached. "My name's Archie Goodwin," I told him. "From Nero Wolfe, on behalf of Lippert, Buff and Assa." There was a chair there, and I sat. "We need to clear up a few little points about the contest."

"Crap," he said.

"That won't do it," I stated. "Not just that one word. Is the contest crap, or am I, or what?"

He shut his eyes. "I'm sick." He opened them. "I'll be all right tomorrow."

"Are you too sick to talk? I don't want to make you worse. I don't know how serious a heart flutter is."

"I haven't got a heart flutter. I've got paroxysmal tachycardia, and it is never serious. I'd be up and around right now if it wasn't for one thing—there are too many fools. The discomfort of paroxysmal tachycardia is increased by fear and anxiety and apprehension and nervousness, and I've got all of 'em on account of fools."

He raised himself on an elbow, reached to the bedstand for a glass of water, drank about a spoonful, and put the glass back. He bounced around and settled on his side, facing me.

"What kind of fools?" I asked politely.

"You're one of 'em. Didn't you come to ask me where I got the gun I shot that man Dahlmann with?"

"No, sir. Speaking for Nero Wolfe, we're not interested in the death of Dahlmann except as it affects the contest and raises points that have to be dealt with."

He snorted: "There you are. Crap. Why should it affect the contest at all? It happened to be last night that someone went there and shot him—some jealous woman or someone who hated him or was afraid of him or wanted to get even with him—and just because it happened last night they think it was connected with the contest. They even think one of us did it. Only a fool would think that. Suppose when he held up that paper, suppose I believed him when he said it was the answers, and I decided to kill

37

him and get it. Finding out where he lived would have been easy enough, even the phone book. So I went there, and getting him to let me in was just as easy, I could tell him there was something about the agreement that I thought ought to be changed and I wanted to discuss it with him. Getting a chance to shoot him might be a little harder, since he might have a faint suspicion I had come to try to get the paper, but it could be managed. So I kill him and take the paper and get back to my hotel room, and where am I?"

I shook my head. "You're telling it."

"I've dug a hole and jumped in. If they go on with the contest on the basis of those answers, I've ruined my chances, because they'll hold us here in the jurisdiction, or if I leave for Chicago before the body is found they'll invite me back and I'll have to come, and if I send in the right answers before my deadline I couldn't explain how I got 'em. If they don't go on with those answers, if they void them and give us new verses, all I've got for killing a man is the prospect of being electrocuted. So they're fools for thinking one of us did it. Crap."

"There's another possibility," I objected. "What if you were a fool yourself? I admit your analysis is absolutely sound, but what if the sight of that paper and the thought of half a million dollars carried you away, and you went ahead and did it and didn't bother with the analysis until afterward? Then when you did realize it and saw where you were, for instance in the District Attorney's office, I should think your heart would flutter no matter what name you gave it. I know mine would."

He turned over on his back and shut his eyes. I sat and looked at him. He was breathing a little faster than normal, and a muscle in his neck twitched a couple of times, but there was no indication of a crisis. I had not scared him to death, and anyway, I had only promised Tim Evarts that I wouldn't find a corpse, not that I wouldn't make one.

He turned back on his side. "For some reason," he said, "I feel like offering you a drink. You look a little like my son-in-law, that may be it. There's a bottle of Scotch in my suitcase that he gave me. Help yourself. I don't want any."

"Thanks, but I guess not. Another time."

38

"As you please. About my being a fool, I was one once, twenty-six years ago, back in nineteen-twenty-nine. I had stacked up a couple of million dollars and it all went. Fifty million others were fools along with me, but that didn't help any. I decided I had had enough and got me a job selling adding machines, and never touched the market again. A few years ago my son-in-law made me quit work because he was doing very well as an architect, and that was all right, I was comfortable, but I always wanted something to do, and one day I saw the advertisement of this contest, and the first thing I knew I was in it up to my neck. I decided to make my daughter and son-in-law a very handsome present."

He coughed, and shut his eyes and breathed a little, then went on. "The point is that it's been twenty-six years since I made a fool of myself, and if you and those other fools only knew it, once was enough. There's only one thing you can tell me that I'm interested in, and that's this, what are they going to do about the contest? As it stands now it's a giveaway, and I'll fight it. That young woman, Susan Tescher—she lives here in New York and she's a researcher for *Clock* magazine. She's working on it right now—and here I am. I'll fight it."

"Fight it how?" I asked.

"That's the question." He passed his finger tips over his right cheek and then over his left one. "I haven't shaved today. I don't see why I shouldn't tell you one idea I had."

"Neither do I."

He had his eyes steady on me, and they didn't look so sick. "You strike me as a sensible young man."

"I am."

"It's just possible that Miss Tescher is a sensible young woman. If she tries to bull it through on the basis of what was agreed last night, after what has happened, she may end up by wishing she'd never heard of the damn contest. I think the rest of us might get together with her and suggest that we split it up five ways. The first five prizes total eight hundred and seventy thousand dollars, so that would make it one hundred and seventy-four thousand apiece. That ought to satisfy everybody, and I don't see why you people would object to it. As it stands now—was that a knock at the door?"

"It sounded like it."

"I told them I didn't want . . . oh well. Come in!"

The door opened slowly and there was Carol Wheelock, without coat or hat. As I left my chair she stopped, and apparently was about to turn and scoot, but I spoke. "Hello there. Come on in."

"Leave the door open," Younger said.

"I'm here," I told him.

"I know you are. With a woman in my hotel room the door stays open."

"I shouldn't have come." She stood. "I should have phoned, but with all the wiretapping—"

"It's all right." I was moving another chair up. "Mr. Younger is resting because he had a little paroxysm, nothing serious."

"Crap," Younger said. "Sit down. I want to talk to you anyway."

She still hesitated, then came on and sat. If she had eaten anything there was no noticeable result. She looked at me. "Does he know about Miss Frazee?"

I shook my head. "I hadn't got to that yet."

She looked at Younger. "I couldn't reach Miss Tescher, and I wanted to speak to you before Mr. Rollins. You know Miss Frazee is the head of the Women's Nature League. You remember it was mentioned last evening, and Mr. Dahlmann was very witty about it. He thought it would be amusing for her to win a prize, and of course she was going to, one of the first five."

"I didn't think he was witty," Younger declared.

She didn't press it. "Well, he thought he was. What I wanted to tell you, three hundred women, members of her league, have been working with Miss Frazee on the contest, and she has sent them the verses we got last night by long distance telephone, and they're working on them now—three hundred of them."

"Just a minute," I put in. "As Mr. Wolfe told you, she said they helped her, but not that they have the new verses. That's an assumption. I admit it has four legs."

Younger had raised himself to an elbow, and the open front of his pajama top showed a hairy chest. "Three hundred women?" he demanded.

"Right. So I doubt if you can sell Miss Frazee on your plan to split it five ways. You'll have to think up—"

40

"Get out!" he commanded. Not me; it was for Mrs. Wheelock. "Get out of here. I'm getting up and I haven't got any pants on. —Wait a minute! You'll be in your room? Stay in your room until you hear from me. I'm going to find Rollins and the three of us are going to fight. We'll blow it so high they won't find any pieces. Stay in your room!"

He gave the covers a kick, proving he had been right about the pants, and she ran. I looked at my watch, and took my hat from the back of the chair.

"I have an appointment," I told him, "and anyway, you're going to be busy."

7

Up in the plant rooms on the roof it was Cattleya mossiae time. In the cool room, the first one you enter from the vestibule, the Odontoglossums were sporting their sprays, and in the middle room, the tropical room, two benches of Phalaenopsis, the hardiest of all to grow well, were crowding the aisle with racemes two feet long, but at mossiae time the big show was in the third room. Of Wolfe's fourteen varieties of mossiae my favorite was reineckiana, with its white, yellow, lilac, and violet. But then, passing through, I only had time for a glance at them.

Wolfe, in the potting-room, washing his hands at the sink and talking with Theodore, growled at me. "Couldn't it wait?"

"Just rhetoric," I said. "It's ten to six and Miss Tescher may be there when you come down, and you might want a report on Younger before you see her. If not, I'll go look at orchids."

"Very well. Since you're here."

I gave it to him verbatim. He had no questions and no comments. By the time I finished he had his hands and nails clean and had moved to the workbench to frown at a bedraggled specimen in a pot.

"Look at this Oncidium varicosum," he grumbled. "Dry rot in April. It has never happened before and there is no explanation. Theodore is certain—"

The buzz of the house phone kept me from learning what Theodore was certain of. Instead, I learned what had upset Fritz downstairs: "Archie, you only told me to admit a Miss Susan Tescher. She has come, but there are three men with her. What do I do?"

"Are they in?"

"Of course not. They're out on the stoop and it has started to rain."

I said I'd be right down, told Wolfe Miss Tescher had arrived with outriders, and beat it. I rarely use the elevator, and never squeeze in together with Wolfe's bulk. Descending the three flights to the main hall, and taking a look through the one-way glass panel, I saw that Fritz's count was accurate. One female and three males were standing in the April shower, glaring in my direction but not seeing me. The men were strangers but not dicks unless they had changed brands without telling me, and it seemed unnecessary to let them get any wetter, so I went and unbolted the door and swung it open, and in they came. A remark about rain being wet might have been expected from the males, but they started removing their coats with no remarks at all. The female said in a clear strong capable voice, "I'm Susan Tescher."

I told her who I was and hung her coat up for her. She was fairly tall, slender but not thin, and not at all poorly furnished with features. From a first glance, and I try to make first glances count, everything about her was smart, with the exception of the earrings, which were enameled clock dials the size of a quarter. She had gray eyes and brassy hair and very good skin and lipstick.

As we were starting for the office the elevator door opened and Wolfe emerged. He stopped, facing her.

"I'm Susan Tescher," she said.

He bowed. "I'm Nero Wolfe. And these gentlemen?"

She used a hand. "Mr. Hibbard, of the legal staff of *Clock*." Mr. Hibbard was tall and skinny. "Mr Schultz, an associate editor of *Clock*." Mr. Schultz was tall and broad. "Mr. Knudsen, a senior editor of *Clock*." Mr. Knudsen was tall and bony.

I had edged on ahead, to be there to get her into the

red leather chair, which was where Wolfe always wanted the target, without any fuss. There was no problem. The men were perfectly satisfied with the three smaller chairs I placed for them, off to my right and facing Wolfe at his desk. All three crossed their legs, settled back, and clasped their hands. When I got out my notebook Schultz called Hibbard's attention, and Hibbard called Knudsen's attention, but there was no comment.

"If you please," Wolfe asked, "in what capacity are these gentlemen present?"

He was looking at them, but Miss Tescher answered. "I suppose you know that I am assistant director of research at *Clock*."

"At least I know it now."

"The publicity about the contest, after what happened last night and this morning, and my connection with it, was discussed at a conference this afternoon. I can tell you confidentially that Mr. Tite himself was there. I thought I would be fired, but Mr. Tite is a very fair man and very loyal to his employees. All my work on the contest was done on my own time—of course I'm a highly trained researcher. So it was decided that Mr. Hibbard and Mr. Knudsen and Mr. Schultz should come with me here. They want to be available for advice if I need it."

"Mr. Hibbard is a counselor-at-law?"

"Yes."

"Is he your attorney?"

"Why—I don't—" She looked at Hibbard. He moved his head, once to the left and back again. "No," she said, "he isn't." She cocked her head. "I want to say something."

"Go ahead."

"I came here only as a favor to Lippert, Buff and Assa, because Mr. Assa asked me to. The conditions for breaking the tie in the contest were agreed to last evening by all of us, and they can be changed only by changing the agreement, and it remains the same. So there is really nothing to discuss. That's the way it looks to me and I wanted you to understand it."

Wolfe grunted. She went on, "But of course there's nothing personal about it—I mean personal towards you. I happen to know a lot about you because I researched you two years ago, when you were on the list of cover prospects for *Clock,* but don't ask me why they didn't use you because I don't know. Of course there are always dozens on the list, and they can't all—"

Knudsen cleared his throat, rather loud, and she looked at him. There was no additional signal that I caught, but evidently she didn't need one. She let it lay. Returning to Wolfe, "So," she said, "it's not personal. It's just that there is nothing to discuss."

"From your point of view," Wolfe conceded, "there probably isn't. And naturally, for you, as a consequence of the peculiar constitution of the human ego, your point of view is paramount. But your ego is bound to be jostled by other egos, and efforts to counteract the jostling by ignoring it have rarely succeeded. It is frequently advisable, and sometimes necessary, to give a little ground. For example, suppose I ask you for information in which you have no monopoly because it is shared with others. Suppose I ask you: at the meeting last evening, after Mr. Dahlmann displayed a paper and said it contained the answers, what remarks were made about it by any of the contestants? What did you say, and what did you hear any of them say?"

"Are you supposing or asking?"

"I'm asking."

She looked at Knudsen. His head moved. At Schultz. His head moved. At Hibbard. His head moved. She returned to Wolfe. "When Mr. Assa asked me to come to see you he said it was about the contest, and that has no bearing on it."

"Then you decline to answer?"

"Yes, I think I should."

"The police must have asked you. Did you decline to answer?"

"I don't think I should tell you anything about what the police asked me or what I said to them."

"Nor, evidently, anything about what the other contestants have said to you or you have said to them."

"My contact with the other contestants has been very limited. Just that meeting last evening."

Wolfe lifted a hand and ran a finger tip along the side of his nose a few times. He was being patient. "I may say, Miss Tescher, that my contact with the other contestants, mine and Mr. Goodwin's, has been a little broader. Several courses have been suggested. One was that all five of you agree that the first five prizes be pooled, and that each of you accept one-fifth of the total as your share. The suggestion was not made by my clients or by me; I am merely asking you, without prejudice, would you consider such a proposal?"

She didn't need guidance on that one. "Of course I wouldn't. Why should I?"

"So you don't concede that the manner of Mr. Dahlmann's death, and the circumstances, call for reconsideration of anything whatever connected with the contest?"

She pushed her head forward, and it reminded me of something, I couldn't remember what. She said slowly and distinctly and positively, "I don't concede anything at all, Mr. Wolfe."

She pulled her head back, and I remembered. A vulture I had seen at the zoo—exactly the same movement. Aside from the movement there was no resemblance; certainly the vulture hadn't looked anything like as smart as she did, and had no lipstick, no earrings, and no hair on its head.

"All the same," Wolfe persisted, "there are the other egos and other viewpoints. I accept the validity of yours, but theirs cannot be brushed aside. Each of you has made a huge investment of time and energy and ingenuity. How much time have you spent on it since the beginning?"

"I don't know. Hundreds and hundreds of hours."

"The rules didn't forbid help. Have you had any?"

"No. A friend of mine with a large library let me use it nights and early mornings before I went to work, but she didn't help. I'm very expert at researching. When they gave me five to do in one week, to break the tie—that was on March twenty-eighth—I took a week off without pay."

Wolfe nodded. "And of course the others made similar sacrifices and endured similar strains. Look at them now. They are detained here willy-nilly, far from their base of operations, by no fault of their own—except possibly for one of them, but that's moot. Whereas you're at home and can proceed as usual. You have an overwhelming advantage and it is fortuitous. Can you pursue it without a qualm? Can you justify it?"

"I don't have to justify it. We made an agreement and

45

I'm not breaking it. And I can't proceed as usual—if I could I'd be at the library now, working. I've got another week off, but I had to spend today with the police and the conference at the office and now here with you. I'll work tonight, but I don't know what tomorrow will be like."

"Would you accept an invitation to meet with the others and discuss a new arrangement?"

"I would not. There's nothing to discuss."

"You are admirably single-minded, Miss Tescher." Wolfe leaned back with his elbows on the chair arms and matched his finger tips. "I must tell you about Miss Frazee—she is in a situation comparable to yours. Her home is in Los Angeles, where three hundred of her friends, fellow members of a league of which she is president, have worked with her on the contest throughout. It is presumed, though not established, that she has telephoned them the verses that were distributed last evening, and that they are busy with them. A situation comparable to yours, though by no means identical. Have you any comment?"

She was staring at him, speechless.

"Because," Wolfe went on, "while there may be no infraction of the rules or the agreement, it is surely an unfair advantage—even against you, since you have already lost a day and there's no telling how much you'll be harassed the rest of the week; but Miss Frazee's friends can proceed unhampered. Don't you think that's worth discussing?"

From the look on Susan's face she would have liked to discuss it with Miss Frazee herself, with fingernails and teeth at ten inches. Before she found any words Knudsen arose, crooked his finger at the other two men and at Susan, and headed for the door. They all got up and followed. Wolfe sat and gazed at their receding backs. Not knowing whether they were adjourning or only taking a recess, I sat pat until I saw that Schultz, out last, was shutting the door to the hall, then I thought I'd better investigate, put down my notebook, went to the door and opened it, and crossed the sill. The quartet was in a close huddle over by the big walnut rack.

"Need any help?" I asked brightly.

"No," Susan said. "We're conferring."

I re-entered the office, closed the door, and told Wolfe, "They're in conference. If I go in the front room and put my ear to the keyhole of the door to the hall I can catch it. After all, it's your house."

'Pfui," he said, and shut his eyes. I treated myself to a good yawn and stretch, and looked at my wrist. Twenty to seven.

For the second time that day we had a king-size wait. At six-forty-five I turned on the radio to see how the Giants had made out with the Phillies, and got no glow out of that. I would have gone to the kitchen for a glass of milk, since dinner would be late, but the only route was through the rear of the hall, and I didn't want to disturb the conference. At six-fifty-five I reminded Wolfe that Harold Rollins was due in five minutes, and he only nodded without opening his eyes. At seven-two the door-bell rang, and I went.

Still in a huddle at the rack, they broke off as I appeared and gave me their faces. Out on the stoop was a lone male. I went on by the huddle, opened the door, and said, "Mr. Rollins? Come in."

My own idea would have been to put him in the front room until the conference was over and we had got the score, but if Wolfe had wanted that he would have said so, and I'm perfectly willing to let him have things his way unless his ego is jostling mine. So I took Rollins' hat and coat and ushered him along to the office. I was inside too and was shutting the door when Susan's voice came. "Mr. Goodwin!"

I pulled the door to with me on the hall side. As I approached she asked, "Wasn't that one of them? The one named Rollins?"

"Right. Harold Rollins, Burlington, Iowa, professor of history at Bemis College."

She looked at her pals. Their heads all moved, an inch to the left and back again. She looked at me. "Mr. Wolfe asked me if I had any comment about what he told me about Miss Frazee. He asked me if I thought it was worth discussing. I have no comment now, but I will have. It's absolutely outrageous to expect—"

A quick tug at her sleeve by Knudsen stopped her. She shot him a glance and then pushed her head forward at

47

me. "No comment!" she shrilled, and turned to reach to the rack for her coat. The men simultaneously reached for theirs.

"If you gentlemen don't mind," I said, perfectly friendly, "my grandmother out in Ohio used to ask me if the cat had my tongue. I've always wondered about it. Was it a cat in your case?"

No soap. Not a peep. I gave up and opened the door to let them out.

8

Back in the office, I attended to the lights before going to my desk. There are eight different lights—one in the ceiling above a big bowl of banded Oriental alabaster, which is on the wall switch, one on the wall behind Wolfe's chair, one on his desk, one on my desk, one flooding the big globe, and three for the book shelves. The one on Wolfe's desk is strictly for business, like crossword puzzles. The one on the wall behind him is for reading. He likes all the others turned on, and after making the rounds I sat, picked up my notebook, and gave Harold Rollins a look.

"They have gone?" Wolfe asked.

"Yes, sir. No comment."

Rollins was comfortable in the red leather chair, right at home, though one about half the size would have been better for him. He hadn't shrunk from underfeeding like Carol Wheelock; he looked healthy enough, what there was of him. Nor was there much to his face except a wide flexible mouth and glasses in thick black frames. You didn't see his nose and chin at all unless you concentrated.

It's hard to tell with glasses like those, but apparently he was returning my regard. "Your name's Goodwin, isn't it?" he asked.

I admitted it.

"Then it was you who sicked that man Younger on me.

You don't expect me to be grateful, do you? I'm not."
He switched to Wolfe. "We might as well start right. I
made this appointment, and kept it, only to pass the time.
I'm in this grotesque imbroglio, with no discoverable
chance of emerging with honor and dignity, so why miss
an opportunity of meeting an eminent bloodhound?" He
smiled and shook his head. "No offense intended. I am
hardly in a position to offend anybody. What are we going to talk about?"

Wolfe was contemplating him. "I suggest, Mr. Rollins,
that your despair is excessive. My client is the firm of
Lippert, Buff and Assa, but in many respects your interest runs with theirs, and their honor and dignity are involved with yours. Both may be salvaged; and in addition,
you may get a substantial amount of money. You didn't
like what Mr. Younger proposed?"

He was still smiling. "Of course I know I should make
allowances."

"For Mr. Younger?"

"For all of you. Your frame of reference is utterly different from mine, in fact to me it seems quite contempt-
ible, but it was my own thoughtlessness that got me
entangled in it. I dug my own grave, that's true; but,
realizing and confessing it, I may still resent the slime and
the worms. Can you get me back my job?"

"Job?"

"Yes. I am a professor of history at Bemis College, but
I won't be very long. It will amuse you to hear—no, that's
not the right way to look at it. It will amuse me to tell
you; that's better. One day last September a colleague
showed me an advertisement of this contest, and said
facetiously that as a student and teacher of history I
should be interested. As a puzzle the thing was so obvious
it was inane, and so was the second one, which my colleague also showed me. I was curious as to how long the
inanity would be maintained, and got others as they appeared, and before long I found I was being challenged.
I made a point of getting them without referring to any
book, but the twelfth one so distracted me that I broke
that ban just to get rid of it."

He screwed up his lips. "Have I said that I hadn't entered the contest?"

"No."

"Well, I hadn't. I regarded it as a diversion, an amusing toy. But after I had solved the twentieth and last, which I must confess was rather ingenious, I sent in an entry blank with my answers. If you were to ask me why I did so I would be at a loss. I suppose in the lower strata of my psyche the primitive lusts are slopping around in the mire, and somehow they managed it; they are not in direct communication with me. The next day I was appalled at what I had done. I had a professorship at the age of thirty-six; I was a serious and able scholar with two books to my credit; and I had well-defined ambitions which I was determined to realize. If I won a prize in a perfume contest—a perfume called *Pour Amour*—it would be a blemish on my career, and if I won a sensational one, a half or a quarter of a million, I would never live it down."

He smiled and shook his head. "But you won't believe I was appalled, because when I was notified that I was in a tie with seventy-one others, and was sent five new verses to solve in a week, I had the answers in four days and sent them in. I can only plead that schizophrenia must have many forms and manifestations, or I could resort to demonology. I was once much impressed by Roskoff's *Geschichte des Teufels*. Anyhow, I sent the answers, and was asked to come to New York, and arrived just twenty-four hours ago; and now I'm involved not only in a perfume contest—Pour Amour Rollins they'll call me—but in a murder, a nationwide *cause célèbre*. I am done for. If I don't resign I'll be fired. Can you get me a job?"

I was wishing he would take his glasses off so I could see his eyes. From his easy posture and his voice and his superior smile he was taking it well, a manly and gallant bozo refusing to squirt blood under the wheels of calamity. But without more sales pressure I wasn't buying the notion that one definition of "calamity" was half a million bucks, even for a man as highly educated as him, and I wanted to see his eyes. All I could see was the reflection of the ceiling light from the lenses.

"You're in a fix," Wolfe admitted, "but I still think your despair is excessive. Establish academic scholarships with your prize money."

"I've thought of that. It wouldn't help much." He

smiled. "The simplest way would be to confess to the murder. That would do it."

"Not without corroboration. Could you furnish any?"

"I'm afraid not. I couldn't describe his apartment, and I don't know what kind of gun was used."

"Then it would be hopeless. Perhaps a better expedient, expose the murderer and become a public hero. The acclaim would smother the infamy. You are not a bloodhound by profession, I know, but you have cerebral resources. You could start by recalling all the details of the meeting last evening. How did they act and talk? What signs of greed or zealotry did they display? Particularly, what did they say and do when Mr. Dahlmann showed the paper and said it was the answers?"

"Nothing. Nothing whatever."

"It was a shock, naturally. But afterward?"

"Not afterward either." The smile was getting more superior. "I would suppose you wouldn't need to be told what the atmosphere was like. We were tigers crouching to spring upon the same prey. Vultures circling to swoop and be first on the carcass to get the heart and liver. The amenities were forced and forged. We separated immediately after the meeting, each clutching his envelope, each wishing the others some crippling misfortune, anything up to death."

"Then you have no idea which of them, if any, thought Mr. Dahlmann was joking."

"Not the faintest."

"Did you?"

"Ah," Rollins looked pleased. "This is more like it, only I thought you would be more subtle. The police wouldn't believe my answer, and you won't either. I really don't know. I was in a sort of nightmare. My demon had brought me there with the single purpose of winning the contest by my own wit and ingenuity. Whether the paper he showed us held the answers or not was a matter of complete indifference to me. If careless chance had put it in my way I would have burned it without looking at it, at the dictate not of conscience, but of pride. I'm sorry to disappoint you, but I can't say if I thought Dahlmann was joking or not because I didn't think one way or the other. Now you want to know what I did last evening after the meeting."

Wolfe shook his head. "Not especially. You have told the police, of course, and they're much better equipped to trace movements and check alibis than I am. And I'm not investigating the murder."

"Exactly what are you doing?"

"I'm trying to find a way to settle the contest in a manner acceptable to all parties. You say Mr. Younger spoke to you? What did he say?"

"He told me what Goodwin told him about Miss Frazee, and he wanted Mrs. Wheelock and me to join him in getting a lawyer and starting legal action. But also he wanted us to propose to Miss Tescher and Miss Frazee that the amount of the first five prizes will be divided equally among us. I told him we couldn't very well do both."

"Which do you prefer?"

"Neither. Since I have to pay the piper I'm going to dance. Dahlmann said these verses are much more obscure than any of the others, and I believe him. I doubt if Miss Frazee's friends can get any of them, and I'll be surprised if Miss Tescher can. When I leave here I'm going to one of the finest private libraries in New York and spend the night there, and I already know which book I'll go to first. This is one of the verses:

> *"From Jack I learned love all the way,*
> *And to the altar would be led;*
> *But on my happy wedding day*
> *I married Charles instead."*

He lifted his hand to his glasses, but only shifted them a little on his nose. "Does that suggest anything to you?"

"No," Wolfe said emphatically.

"It does to me. Not any detail of it, but the flavor. I have no idea what her name was, but I think I know where to find her. I may be wrong, but I doubt it, and if not, there's one right off."

He probably had it. Either he had had a lucky hunch, or he knew a lot about flavors, or he had got the paper from Dahlmann's wallet and was preparing the ground for a later explanation of how and where he got the answers. I could certainly have impressed him by asking if the book he would go to first would be Jacques Casanova's *Memoirs*, but he might have suspected me if I had also told him her name was Christine and he should try Volume Two, pages one hundred seventy-two to two hundred one, of the Adventuros edition.

Wolfe said abruptly, "Then I mustn't keep you, if you're going to work. I wouldn't care to stir the choler of a demon." He put his hands on the desk edge to push his chair back, and arose. "I hope to see you again, Mr. Rollins, but I shall try to interfere as little as may be with your labors. You will excuse me." He headed for the door and was gone.

Rollins looked at me. "What was that, pique? Or did I betray myself and he has gone for handcuffs?"

"Forget it." I stood up. "Don't you smell anything?"

He sniffed. "Nothing in particular. What is it?"

"Of course," I conceded, "you're not a bloodhound. It's shad roe in casserole with parsley, chervil, shallot, marjoram, bay leaf, and cream. That's his demon, or one of them. He has an assortment. You're going? If you don't mind, what was Number Nine? I think it was. It goes:

> *"By the law himself had earlier made*
> *I could not be his legal wife;*
> *The law he properly obeyed*
> *And loved me all my life."*

He had turned at the door, and his smile was super-superior. "That was palpable. Aspasia and Pericles."

"Oh, sure. I should have known."

We went to the hall and I held his coat. As I opened the door he inquired, "Wasn't that Miss Tescher here when I came?"

I told him yes.

"Who were the three men?"

"Advisers she brought along. You should have heard them. They talked Mr. Wolfe into a corner."

He thought he was going to ask me more, vetoed it, and went. I shut the door and started for the kitchen to tell Wolfe about Aspasia and Pericles, but the phone ringing pulled me into the office. I answered it, had a brief exchange with the caller, and then went to the kitchen, where Wolfe was in conference with Fritz, and told him:

"Talbott Heery will be here at a quarter past nine."

Already on edge, he roared. "I will not gallop through my dinner!"

I told him, apologetically, that I was afraid he'd have to. He only had an hour and a half.

9

The subject of discussion at Wolfe's dinner table, whether we had company or not, might be anything from politics to polio, so long as it wasn't current business. Business was out. That evening was no exception, strictly speaking, but it came close. Apparently at some time during the day Wolfe had found time to gallop through the encyclopedia article on cosmetics, and at dinner he saw fit, intermittently, to share it with me. He started, when we had finished the chestnut soup and were waiting for Fritz to bring the casserole, by quoting verbatim a bill which he said had been introduced into the English Parliament in 1770. It ran, he said:

"All women of whatever age, rank, profession, or degree, whether virgins, maids, or widows, that shall, from and after this Act, impose upon, seduce, and betray into matrimony, any of His Majesty's subjects, by the scents, paints, cosmetic washes, artificial teeth, false hair, Spanish wool, iron stays, hoops, high heeled shoes, bolstered hips, shall incur the penalty of the law in force against witchcraft and like misdemeanors and the marriage, upon conviction, shall stand null and void."

I asked him what Spanish wool was, and had him. He didn't know, and because he can't stand not knowing the meaning of any word or phrase he sees or hears, I asked why he hadn't looked in the dictionary, and he said he had but it wasn't there. Another item was that Mary Queen of Scots bathed in wine regularly, and so did the elder ladies of the court, but the younger ones couldn't afford it and had to use milk. Another was that when they found unguent vases in old Egyptian tombs they had dug into, the aromatics in them were still fragrant, after thirty-five hundred years. Another, that Roman fashion leaders at the time of Caesar's wife bleached their hair with a kind of soap that came from Gaul. Another, that Napoleon liked Josephine to use cosmetics and got them for her from Martinique. Another, that Cleopatra and other Egyptian babes painted the under side of their eyes green, and the lid, lashes, and eyebrows black. For the black they used kohl, and put it on with an ivory stick.

I admitted it was very interesting, and made no remark about how helpful it would be in finding out who swiped Dahlmann's wallet, since that would have touched on business. Even after we finished with cheese and coffee and left the dining room to cross the hall to the office, I let him digest in peace, and went to my desk and dialed Lily Rowan's number. When I told her I wouldn't be able to make it to the Polo Grounds tomorrow, she began to call Wolfe names, and thought of several new ones that showed her wide experience and fine feeling for words. While we were talking the doorbell rang, but Fritz had been told about Heery, so I went ahead and finished the conversation properly. When I hung up and swiveled, Heery was in the red leather chair.

He measured up to it, both vertically and horizontally, much better than either Rollins or Mrs. Wheelock. In a dinner jacket, with the expanse of white shirt front, he looked broader even than before. Apparently he had been glancing around, for he was saying, "This is a very nice room. Very personal. You like yellow, don't you?"

"Evidently," Wolf muttered. Such remarks irritate him. Since the drapes and couch cover and cushions and five visible chairs were yellow, it did seem a little obvious.

"Yellow is a problem," Heery declared. "It has great advantages, but also it has a lot of drawbacks. Yellow streak. Yellow journalism. Yellow fever. It's very popular for packaging, but Louis Dahlmann wouldn't let me use it. Formerly I used it a great deal. Seeing all your yellow made me think of him."

"I doubt," Wolfe said drily, "if you needed my décor to remind you of Mr. Dahlmann at this juncture."

"That's funny," Heery said, perfectly serious.

"It wasn't meant to be."

"Anyway, it is, because it's wrong. That's the first time I've thought of him today. Ten seconds after I heard he was dead, and how he had died, I was in a stew about the effect on the contest and my business, and I'm still in it. I haven't had any room for thinking about Louis Dahlmann. Have you seen all the contestants?"

"Four of them. Mr. Goodwin saw Mr. Younger."

"Have you got anywhere?"

Wolfe hated to work right after dinner. He said testily, "I report only to my client, Mr. Heery."

"That's funny too. Your client is Lippert, Buff and Assa. I'm one of their biggest accounts—their commission on my business last year was over half a million. I'm paying all the expenses of the contest, and of course the prizes. And you won't even tell me if you've got anywhere?"

"Certainly not." Wolfe frowned at him. "Are you really as silly as you sound? You know quite well what my obligation to my client is. You have a simple recourse: get one of them on the phone and have me instructed—preferably Mr. Buff or Mr. Assa."

It seemed a good spot for Heery to offer to knock his block off, but instead he got to his feet, stuck his hands in his pockets, and looked around, apparently for something to look at, for he marched across to the globe and stood there staring at it. His back looked even broader than his front. Pretty soon he turned and came back and sat down.

"Have they paid you a retainer?" he asked.

"No, sir."

He took a thin black leather case from his breast pocket, opened it and tore off a strip of blue paper, produced a midget fountain pen, put the paper on the table at his elbow, and wrote. After putting the pen and case away he reached to send the paper fluttering onto Wolfe's desk and said, "There's ten thousand dollars. I'm your client now, or my firm is. If you want more say so."

Wolfe reached for the check, tore it across, again, again, and leaned to the right to drop it in the wastebasket. He straightened up. "Mr. Heery. I am never too complaisant when my digestion is interrupted, and you are trying me. You might as well go."

I'll be damned if Heery didn't look at me. Wanting to

56

save him the embarrassment of offering me a twenty, possibly even a C, to put him back on the track, and getting another turndown, and also thinking that if Wolfe wanted his nose pushed in I might as well help, I met his eyes and told him, "When you do go, if you're still looking for a better time and place there's a little yard out back."

He burst out laughing—a real good hearty laugh. He stopped long enough to say, "You're a team, you two," and then laughed some more. We sat and looked at him. He took out a folded handkerchief and coughed into it a couple of times, and was sober.

"All right," he said, "I'll tell you how it is."

"I know how it is." Wolfe was good and sore.

"No, you don't. I went about it the wrong way, so I'll start over. LBA has a good deal at stake in this mess, I know that, but I have more. If this contest explodes in my face it could ruin me. Will you listen?"

Wolfe was leaning back with his eyes closed. "I'm listening," he muttered.

"You have to know the background. I started my business twenty years ago on a shoestring. I worked hard, but I had some luck, and my biggest piece of luck was that a man named Lippert, an advertising man, got interested. The firm's name then was McDade and Lippert. My product was good, but Lippert was better than good, he was great, and in ten years my company was leading the field in dollar volume. It was sensational. Then Lippert died. Momentum kept us on the rise for a couple of years, and then we started to sag. Not badly, we had some ups too, but it was mostly downs. I still had a good organization and a good product, but Lippert was gone, and that was the answer."

He looked at his folded handkerchief as if he wondered what it was for, and stuck it back in his pocket. "In nineteen-fifty the LBA people submitted some names for a new line we were getting ready to start, and from the list I picked Pour Amour. I didn't learn until later that that name had been suggested by a young man named Louis Dahlmann who hadn't been with them long. Do you know anything about the agency game?"

"No."

"It's very tough, especially with the big ones. The men

who have made it, who have got up around the top, most of them spend a lot of their time kicking the faces of the ones who are trying to climb. Of course that's more or less true in any game because it's how people are made, but advertising agencies are about the worst, I mean the big ones. It took me two years to find out who thought of that name Pour Amour, and it was another year before Dahlmann was allowed to confer with me on my account. By that time he had shown so much stuff there was no holding him. There was a lot of talk—you may have heard of him?"

"No."

"He wasn't very likable. He was too cocky, and if he thought you were a goddam fool he said so, but he had real brains and there's no substitute for brains, and his were a special kind. I don't say that Oliver Buff and Pat O'Garro and Vern Assa haven't got brains. Buff has some real ability. He's a good front man. Lippert trained him and knew what he was good for. Now he's the senior member of the firm. For presenting an outline for an institutional campaign to the heads of a big national corporation, he's as good as anybody and better than most, but that kind of approach never has sold cosmetics and never will. I've been one of the firm's big accounts for years, and he has never personally come up with an idea that was worth a dime."

Heery turned a hand over. "There's Pat O'Garro. He knows about as much about advertising, my kind, as I know about Sanskrit, but he's at the very top as a salesman. He could sell a hot-water bottle to a man on his way to hell, and most of the accounts LBA has today, big and little, were landed by him, but that's nothing in my pocket. I don't need someone to sell me on LBA, I need someone who can keep my products sliding over the counters from Boston to Los Angeles and New Orleans to Chicago, and O'Garro's not the man. Neither is Vern Assa. He started in as a copy writer, and that's where he shines. He has a big reputation, and now he's a member of the firm—so is O'Garro of course. I did a lot of analyzing of Vern and his stuff during the years after Lippert died, and it had real quality. I recognize that, but there was something lacking—the old Lippert touch wasn't there. It's not just words, you've got to have

58

ideas before you're ready for words, and LBA didn't have any that were worth a damn until Louis Dahlmann came along."

He shook his head. "I thought my worries were over for good. I admit I didn't like him, but there are plenty of people to like. He was young, and within a year he would have been a member of the firm—he could have forced it whenever he pleased—and before too long he would be running the show, and he had a real personal interest in my account because it appealed to him. Now he's dead, and I'm through with LBA. I've decided on that, I'm through with them, but this goddam contest mess has got to be cleaned up. This morning, when they suggested hiring you, I didn't have my thoughts in order and I told them to go ahead, but with the situation the way it is and me deciding to cut loose from them as soon as this is straightened out it doesn't make sense for LBA to be your client. It will be my money you'll get anyhow. You were a little too quick tearing up that check."

"Not under the circumstances," Wolfe said.

"You didn't know all the circumstances. Now you do—at least the main points. Another point, some important decision about this contest thing may have to be made at any minute, and be made quick, about what you do or don't do, and as it stands now they hired you and they'll decide it. I won't have it that way. I've got more at stake than they have." He took the black leather case from his pocket. "What shall I make it? Ten thousand all right?"

"It can't be done that way," Wolfe objected. "You know it can't. You have a valid point, but you admit you told them to come and hire me. There's a simple way out: get them on the phone and tell them you wish to replace them as my client, and if they acquiesce they can speak to me and tell me so."

Heery looked at him. He put his palms on the chair arms, and spread his fingers and held them stiff. "That would be difficult," he said. "My relations with them the past year or so, especially Buff, have been a little—" He let it hang, and in a moment finished positively, "No, I can't do that."

Wolfe grunted. "I might be willing to phone them myself and tell them what you want. At your request."

"That would be just as bad. It would be worse. You

understand, I've got to avoid an open break right now."

"I suppose so. Then I'm afraid you'll have to accept the status quo. I have sympathy with your position, Mr. Heery. Your interest is as deeply engaged as theirs, and as you say, the money they pay me will have come from you. At a minimum you have a claim to get my reports firsthand. Do you want me to phone them for authority to give them to you? That shouldn't be an intolerable strain on the thread of your relations. I shall tell them that it seems to me your desire is natural and proper."

"It would be something," Heery said grudgingly.

"Shall I proceed?"

"Yes."

The phone rang. I answered it, exchanged some words with the caller, asked him to hold on, and turned to tell Wolfe that Rudolph Hansen wished to speak to him. He reached for his instrument, changed his mind, left his chair, and made for the door. As he rounded the corner of his desk he pushed air down with his palm, which meant that I was to hang up when he was on—presumably to leave me free to chat with the company. A faint squeak that came via the hall reminded me that I had forgotten to oil the kitchen door. When I heard Wolfe's voice in my ear I cradled the phone.

Heery and I didn't chat. He looked preoccupied, and I didn't want to take his mind off his troubles. We passed some minutes in silent partnership before Wolfe returned, crossed to his chair, and sat.

He addressed Heery. "Mr. Hansen was with Mr. Buff, Mr. O'Garro, and Mr. Assa. They wanted my report and I gave it to them. They have no objection to my reporting to you freely, at any time."

"That's damned sweet of them," Heery said, not appreciatively. "Did *they* have anything to report?"

"Nothing of any consequence."

"Then I'm back where I started. Have you got anywhere?"

"Now I can answer you. No."

"Why not?"

Wolfe stirred. "Mr. Heery. I tell you precisely what I told Mr. Hansen. If my talks with the contestants had led me to any conclusions, I might be ready to disclose them and I might not, but I have formed no conclusions.

Conjectures, if I have any, are not fit matter for a report unless I need help in testing them, and I don't. You interrupted the digestion not only of my dinner, but also of the information and impressions I have gathered in a long and laborious day. Those four men wanted to come here. I told them either to let me alone until I have something worth discussing or hire somebody else."

"But there's no time! What do you do next?"

It took another five minutes to get rid of him, but finally he went. After escorting him to the door I went back to my desk, got at the typewriter, and resumed where I had left off on my notes of the Frazee interview. They should all be done before I went to bed, and it was after ten o'clock, so I hammered away. There were one or two remarks I had for Wolfe, and several questions I wanted to ask, but I was too busy, and besides, he was deep in a book. When I returned after seeing Heery out he had already been to the bookshelves and was back at his desk, with *Beauty for Ashes,* by Christopher La Farge, opened to his place, and the wall light turned on. That may not be the way you go about settling down to work on a hard job with a close deadline, but you're not a genius.

I had finished Frazee and was well along with Wheelock when the doorbell rang. As I started for the hall I offered five to one that it was LBA and their lawyer, disregarding Wolfe's demand to be let alone, but I was wrong. When I flipped the switch of the stoop light, one glance through the panel was enough. Stepping back into the office, I told Wolfe:

"Too bad to disturb you—"

"No one," he growled. "No one on earth."

"Okay. It's Cramer."

He lowered the book, with his lips tightened. Slowly and neatly, he dog-eared a page and closed the book on the desk. "Very well," he said grimly. "Let him in."

The doorbell rang again.

10

Wolfe and Inspector Cramer of Manhattan Homicide West have never actually come to blows, though there have been times when Cramer's big red seamy face has gone almost white, and his burly broad shoulders have seemed to shrink, under the strain. I can always tell what the tone is going to be, at least for the kickoff, by the way he greets me when I let him in. If he calls me Archie, which doesn't happen often, he wants something he can expect to get only as a favor and has determined to forget old sores and keep it friendly. If he calls me Goodwin and asks how I am, he still is after a favor but thinks he is entitled to it. If he calls me Goodwin but shows no interest in my health, he has come for what he would call co-operation and intends to get it. If he calls me nothing at all, he's ready to shoot from the hip and look out.

That time it wasn't Archie, but he asked how I was, and after he got into the red leather chair he accepted an offer of beer from Wolfe, and apologized for coming so late without phoning. As Fritz served the beer I went to the kitchen to get a glass of milk for myself. When I returned Cramer had a half-empty glass in his hand and was licking foam from his lips.

"I hope," he said, "that I didn't interrupt anything important." He was gruff, but he would be gruff saying his prayers.

"I'm on a case," Wolfe said, "and I was working." *Beauty for Ashes,* by Christopher La Farge, is a novel written in verse, the scene of the action being Rhode Island. I don't read novels in verse, but I doubt if there's anything in it about perfume contests, or even any kind of cosmetics. If it were *Ashes for Beauty* that might have been different.

"Yeah," Cramer said. "The Dahlmann murder."

"No, sir." Wolfe poured beer. "I'm aware of your disapproval of private detectives concerning themselves with murders in your jurisdiction—heaven knows I should be —and it pleases me to know that I'm not incurring it. I am not investigating a murder."

"That's fine. Would you mind telling me who your client is? This case you're on?"

"As a boon?"

"I don't care what you call it, just tell me."

"There's no reason why I shouldn't, in confidence of course. A firm, an advertising agency, called Lippert, Buff and Assa."

I raised my brows. Evidently Cramer wasn't the only one in favor of favors. Wolfe was being almost neighborly.

"I've heard of them," Cramer said. "Just today, in fact. That's the firm Louis Dahlmann was with."

"That's right."

"When did they hire you?"

"Today."

"Uh-huh. And also today four people have come to see you, not counting your clients, who were at a dinner meeting with Dahlmann last night, and Goodwin has called on another one at his hotel. But you're not investigating a murder?"

"No, sir."

"Nuts."

It looked as if the honeymoon was over and before long fur would be flying, but Cramer took the curse off his lunge with a diversion. He drank beer, and put his empty glass down. "Look," he said, "I've heard you do a lot of beefing about people being rational. Okay. If anyone who knew you, and knew who has been coming here today— if her didn't think you were working on the murder would he be rational? You know damn well he wouldn't. I'm being rational. If you want to try to talk me out of it, go ahead."

Wolfe made a noise which he may have thought was a friendly chuckle. "That would be a new experience, Mr. Cramer. There have been times when I have tried to talk you *into* being rational. I can only tell you, also in confidence, what my job is. Of course you know about the perfume contest, and about the wallet that was missing from Mr. Dahlmann's pocket. I'm going to provide for a satisfactory settlement of the contest by learning who took the wallet, and what was in it, to demonstrate that none of its contents had any bearing on the contest. I'm also going to arrange that certain events, especially the detention of four of the contestants in New York, shall not prevent the fair and equitable distribution of the prizes. If you ask why I'm being so outspoken with you, it's because our interests touch but do not conflict. If and when I get anything you might need you shall have it."

"Quite a job." Cramer was eying him, not as a neighbor. "How are you going to learn who took the wallet without tagging the murderer?"

"Perhaps I can't. That's where our interests touch. But the murder is not my concern."

"I see. Just a by-product. And you say that the paper Dahlmann showed them and put back in his wallet didn't have the answers on it."

"Well." Wolfe pursed his lips. "Not categorically. On that point I am restrained. That is what my clients have told you, and it would be uncivil for me to contradict them. In any case, that illustrates the difference between your objective and mine. Since one of my purposes is to achieve a fair and satisfactory distribution of the prizes, the contents of that paper are of the first importance to me. But to you, that is of no importance at all. What matters to you is not whether the paper contained the answers, but whether the contestants thought it did. If you had good evidence that one of them thought that Dahlmann was only hoaxing them, you'd have to eliminate him as a suspect. By the way, have you any such evidence?"

"No. Have you?"

"No, sir. I have no evidence of anything whatever."

"Do you believe that one of the contestants killed him?"

Wolfe shook his head. "I've told you, I'm not working on a murder. I think it likely that one of them took the wallet—only a conjecture, not a belief."

"Are you saying there might have been two of them—one killed him and one took the wallet?"

"Not at all. Of course my information is scanty. I haven't even read the account in the evening paper, knowing it couldn't be relied on. Have you reason to think there were two?"

"No."

"You are assuming that whoever killed him took the wallet?"

"Yes."

"Then so am I. As I said, there's no conflict. You agree?"

There was some beer left in Cramer's bottle, and he poured it, waited a little for the foam to go down, drank, put the glass down, and licked his lips.

He looked at Wolfe. "I'll tell you. I have never yet bumped into you in the course of my duties without conflict before I was through, but I don't say it couldn't possibly happen. As it stands now, if I take you at your word —I say if—I think we might get along. I think your clients are holding out on us. I think they're worried more about what happens to their goddam contest than what happens to a murderer, and that's why I'm willing to believe your job is what you say it is. I think they have probably given it to you straight, and I'd like to know exactly what they've told you, but I certainly don't expect you to tell me. I think that on the contest part, especially the paper Dahlmann had in his wallet, you're on the inside track, and you know things or you'll learn things we don't know and maybe can't learn. God knows I don't expect to pump them out of you, but I do expect you to realize that it won't hurt you a damn bit to loosen up with anything I could use."

"It's a pity," Wolfe said.

"What's a pity?"

"That you choose this occasion for an appeal instead of the usual bludgeon, because this time I'm armored. Mr. Rudolph Hansen, who is a member of the bar, made our conversation a privileged communication by taking a dollar from me as a retainer. I'm his client. It's a pity you don't give me a chance to raise my shield."

Cramer snorted. "A lot you need it. I've had enough goes at you without a shield. But this is a new one. You can't tell me anything because it's all privileged, huh?"

"No, sir." Wolfe was a little hurt. "I acquiesced in Mr. Hansen's subterfuge only to humor him. What I was told under the cloak of privilege may be of help in connection with the contest, but it wouldn't help you to find the murderer—since you know about the wallet and the paper. The same is true of my conversations with the contestants, except to add that I have not been led to conclude that any one of them did not take the wallet. I think any one of them might have done so, and, as a corollary, might have killed Dahlmann to get it. Beyond that I have nothing but a medley of conjectures which I was sorting out when you interrupted me. None of them is worth discussing—at least not until I look them over. I'll make this engagement: when I reach an assumption I like you'll hear from me before I act on it. Meanwhile, it would simplify matters if I knew a few details."

"Yeah. You haven't even read the papers?"

"No, sir."

"I'll be glad to save you the trouble and maybe throw in a few extras. He was killed between eleven-thirty and three o'clock, shot once from behind, with a cushion for a muffler, with a .32 revolver. That's from the bullet; we haven't found the gun. The building has a self-service elevator and no doorman, and we haven't dug up anyone who saw Dahlmann come home or saw anyone else coming to see him. Do you want all the negatives?"

"I like positives better."

"So do I, but we haven't got any, or damn few. No fingerprints that have helped so far, no other clues from the premises, nothing in his papers or other effects, no hackie that took somebody there, no phone call to that number from the hotel, and so on right through the routine. But you already knew that. If routine had got us anywhere I wouldn't be here keeping you from your work."

"Your routine is impeccable," Wolfe said politely.

"Much obliged. As for alibis, nobody is out completely. Getting out of a big hotel, and back in again, without being observed, isn't hard to do if you've got a good reason for it. The Tescher woman says that after the meeting she went to the library of a friend of hers and worked there on the contest until four o'clock, but nobody was in the room with her and everyone in the house was asleep. This leads to the point that really brought me here—the chief point. We're finding out that there were quite a few people around town who had it in for Louis Dahlmann—three or more women for personal reasons, two or three men for personal reasons, and several of both sexes for business reasons. Even some of his own business associates. We're looking into them, checking on where they were last night and so on, but the fact that his wallet was taken, and nothing else, may mean that it's a waste of time and talent. There was no money in the wallet; he carried bills in a roll in another pocket. The wallet was more of a card case, driver's license and so on."

Speaking of pockets must have reminded him. He reached to his breast pocket and took out a cigar, and wrapped his fingers around it. "So," he said, "I thought you might answer a question. Now that you've told me what you're after, I think so even more. Was he killed in order to get the wallet, or not? If so, it was one of the contestants and we can more or less forget the others, for now anyway, and it was on account of the contest, and as I said, you've got the inside track on that. I'm not asking for Goodwin's notes of your talk with your clients and that lawyer. I'm only asking your opinion, if he was killed to get the wallet."

"I repeat, Mr. Cramer, I am not investigating the murder."

"Damn it, who said you were? How do you want me to put it?"

Wolfe's shoulders went up and down. "It doesn't matter. You only want my opinion. I am strongly inclined to think that your man, the murderer, and my man, the thief, are one and the same. It would seem to follow, therefore, that the answer to your question is yes. Does that satisfy you?"

From the look on Cramer's face, it didn't. "I don't like that 'strongly inclined,'" he objected. "You know damn well what's on my mind. And this privileged communication dodge. Why couldn't it be like this: after the meeting last night Dahlmann's associates talked it over, and they decided it was dangerous for him to have that paper in his wallet, and one of them went to his place to get it or dsetroy it. When he got there the door wasn't locked, and he went in and found Dahlmann on the floor, dead. He took the wallet from his pocket and beat it. Don't ask me why he didn't notify the police, ask him; he could have thought he would be suspected. Anyhow he didn't, but of course he had to tell his associates, and they all got hold of their lawyer and told him, and after talking it over they decided to hire you."

"To do what?"

"To figure out a way of handling it so the contest wouldn't blow them all sky high. Of course the contestants would learn not only that Dahlmann had been killed but also that the wallet was missing, and they would suspect each other of getting the answers, and it would be a hell of a mess. But I'm not going to try to juggle that around, that's their lookout, and yours. My lookout is that if it happened that way the contestants are not my meat at all because he wasn't killed to get the wallet. And can you give me a reason why it couldn't have happened that way?"

"No, sir."

"And the lawyer fixing it so that what he told you was privileged—wouldn't that fit in?"

"Yes," Wolfe conceded. "But it is a fact, not an opinion, that if it did happen that way I am not privy to it. I have been told that none of Mr. Dahlmann's associates went to his apartment last night, and have had no reason to suspect that they were gulling me. If they were they're a pack of fools."

"You state that as a fact."

"I do."

"Well," Cramer allowed, "it's not your kind of a lie." He was suddenly flustered, realizing that wasn't the way to keep it clean. He blurted, "You know what I mean." He stuck the cigar between his teeth and chewed on it. If he couldn't chew Wolfe the cigar would have to do. I've never seen him light one.

"Yes," Wolfe said indulgently, "I know what you mean."

Cramer took the cigar from his mouth. "You asked me a while ago if I assumed that whoever killed him took the wallet, and I said yes, but I should have said maybe. This other angle has got a bite. If I got some grounds to believe that one or more of Dahlmann's associates went to his place last night that would make it a different story entirely, because that would account for the missing wallet, and I could stop concentrating on the contestants. I tell you frankly I have no such grounds. None of them— Buff, O'Garro, Assa, Heery, Hansen the lawyer—no one of that bunch can prove he didn't go down to Perry Street some time last night, but I haven't got anything to back

68

up a claim that one of them did. You understand I'm not itching to slap a murder charge on him; as I said, he could have found Dahlmann dead and took the wallet. In that case he would be the one you're interested in, and I'd have an open field to find the murderer."

"Satisfactory all around," Wolfe said drily.

"Yeah. You say if one of them went there last night you know nothing about it, and I believe you, but what if they held that out on you? Wouldn't they? Naturally?"

"Not if they expected me to earn my fee." Wolfe looked up at the clock. "It's midnight. Mr. Cramer. I can only say that I reject your theory utterly. Not only for certain reasons of my own—as you say, I'm on the inside track on the contest—but also from other considerations. If one of those men went there last night and found Dahlmann dead, why was he ass enough to take the wallet, when he knew it would be missed, and that that would make a botch of the contest? He had to have the paper, of course, since if it were left on the corpse it would be seen by policemen, and possibly by reporters too, but why didn't he just take the paper and leave the wallet?"

"By God," Cramer said, "you were lying after all."

"Yes? Why?"

"Because that's dumb and you're not dumb. He goes in and finds a corpse, and he's nervous. It makes people nervous to find a corpse. He wants to turn and run like hell, they all do, especially if there's the slightest reason for them to be suspected, but he makes himself get the wallet from the corpse's pocket. He may even intend to take the paper and put the wallet back and start looking for the paper, but he thinks of fingerprints. Maybe he can wipe the wallet off before he puts it back, but he might miss one. Even so, he might try, if he calmly considered all the consequences of taking the wallet, but he's not calm and there's no time and he has to get out of there. So he gets, with the wallet. Excuse me for taking up your valuable time with kindergarten stuff, but you asked for it."

He stood up, looked at the cigar in his hand, threw it at my wastebasket, and missed. He glared at it and then at Wolfe. "If that's the best you can do I'll be going." He turned.

"Manifestly," Wolfe said, "you don't believe Mr. Hansen and the others when they profess their conviction that Mr. Dahlmann's display of the paper was only a hoax?"

Cramer turned at the door long enough to growl, "Nuts. Do you?"

When I returned to the office after seeing him out Wolfe was still at his desk, pinching the lobe of his ear with a thumb and forefinger, staring át nothing. I put my empty milk glass on one of the beer trays, took them to the kitchen, washed and wiped the glasses, disposed of the bottles, and put the trays away. Fritz goes to bed at eleven unless he has been asked not to. Back in the office, the ear massage was still under way. I spoke. "I can finish the typing tonight if there are other errands for the morning. Have I got a program?"

"No."

"Oh well," I said cheerfully, "there's no rush. April twentieth is a week off. You can read twenty books in a week."

He grunted. "Get Saul and ask him to breakfast with me in my room at eight o'clock. Give me two hundred dollars for him—no, make it three hundred—and lock the safe and go to bed. I want some quiet."

I obeyed, of course, but I wondered. Could he be tossing a couple of C's—no, three—of LBA money to the breeze just to make me think he had hatched something? Saul Panzer was the best man in the city of New York for any kind of a job, but what was it? Tailing five people, hardly. If tailing one, who and why? If not tailing, then what? For me, nothing we had heard or seen had pointed in anyone's direction. For him, I didn't believe it. He wanted company for breakfast, and not me. Okay.

I got Saul at his apartment on East Thirty-eighth Street, signed him up for the morning, got the money from the cash drawer in the safe and locked the safe, gave Wolfe the dough, and asked him, "Then I don't do the typing tonight?"

"No. Go to bed. I have work to do."

I went. Up one flight I stopped on the landing, thinking it might help if I tiptoed back down and went in and caught him with his book up, but decided it would only make him so stubborn he'd read all night.

11

My morning paper is usually the *Times*, with the *Gazette* for a side dish, but that Thursday I gave the *Gazette* a bigger play because it has a keener sense of the importance of homicide. Its by-line piece on the career and personality of the brilliant young advertising genius who had been shot in the back did not say that there were at least a hundred beautiful and glamorous females in the metropolitan area who might have had reason to erase him, but it gave that impression without naming names.

However, that was only a tactful little bone tossed to the sex hounds for them to gnaw on. The main story was the contest, and they did it proud, with their main source of information Miss Gertrude Frazee of Los Angeles. There was a picture of her on page three which made her unique combination of rare features more picturesque than in the flesh, and harder to believe. She had briefed the reporter thoroughly on the Women's Nature League, told him all about the dinner meeting Tuesday evening, including Dahlmann's display of the paper and what he said, and spoken at length of her rights as a contestant under the rules and the agreement.

Of the other contestants, Susan Tescher of *Clock* magazine had been inaccessible to journalists, presumably after consulting her three windbags. Harold Rollins had been reached but had refused any information or comment; he hadn't even explained why winning half a million bucks would be a fatal blow to him. Mrs. Wheelock, who was living on pills, and Philip Younger, who had paroxysms to contend with, had apparently been almost as talkative as Miss Frazee. They were both indignant, bitter, and pugnacious, but on one point their minds had not met. Younger thought that the only fair way out of the mess was to split the prize money five ways, whereas Mrs. Wheelock did not. She was holding out for the big one, and said the five verses should be scrapped and five new ones substituted, under circumstances that would give each of them an equal opportunity.

Perhaps I should have confined my reading to the contest part, since we hadn't been hired for the murder, but only Fritz was in the kitchen with me and he wouldn't blab. There were a lot of facts that Cramer hadn't furnished—that Dahlmann was wearing a dark blue suit; that he had taken a taxi from the Churchill to his apartment and arrived a little before 11:30; that the woman who found him when she came to get his breakfast was named Elga Johnson; that his apartment was two rooms and bath; that the bullet had hit a rib after passing through the heart; and many other details equally helpful. The name of the murderer wasn't given.

Having got an early start, I was through with breakfast and the papers and was in the office at the typewriter when Saul Panzer came. Saul is not a natural for Mr. America. His nose is twice as big as he needs, he never looks as if he had just shaved, one shoulder is half an inch higher than the other and they both slope, and his coat sleeves are too short. But if and when I find myself up a tree with a circle of man-eating tigers crouching on the ground below, and a squad of beavers starting to gnaw at the trunk of the tree, the sight of Saul approaching would be absolutely beautiful. I have never seen him fazed.

He came at eight sharp and went right upstairs, and I went back to the typewriter. At five to nine he came back down but I didn't hear him until he called to me from the door to the hall. "Want to come and bolt me out?"

I swiveled. "With pleasure. That's what the bolt's for, such as you." I arose. "Have a good breakfast?"

"You know I did."

I was with him. "Need any professional coaching?"

"I sure do." He was at the rack getting his things. "I'll start at the bottom and work down."

"That's the spirit." I opened the door. "If you get your throat cut or something just give me a ring."

"Glad to, Archie. You'd be the one all right."

"Okay. Keep your gloves on."

He went, and I shut the door and went back to work. There had been a day when I got a little peeved if Wolfe gave Saul a chore without telling me what it was, and also told him not to tell me, but that was long past. It didn't

72

peeve me any more; it merely bit me because I couldn't guess it. I sat at my desk a good ten minutes trying to figure it, then realized that was about as useful as reading a novel in verse, and hit the typewriter.

My speed at typing notes of interviews depends on the circumstances. Once in a real pinch I did ten pages an hour for three hours, but my average is around six or seven, and I have been known to mosey along at four or five. That morning I stepped on it, to get as much done as possible before Wolfe came down from the plant rooms at eleven o'clock, since he would certainly have some errands ready for me. I was interrupted by phone calls— one from Rudolph Hansen, wanting a progress report, one from Oliver Buff, wanting the same, one from Philip Younger, wanting me to arrange an appointment for him with the LBA crowd and getting sore when I stalled him, and one from Lon Cohen of the *Gazette,* wanting to know if I felt like giving him something hot on the Dahlmann murder. Being busy, I didn't start an argument by saying we weren't working on the murder; I just told him he'd have to stand in line, and didn't bother to ask him how he knew we were in the play. Probably Miss Frazee. In spite of the interruptions, I had finished Wheelock and Younger and Tescher by eleven o'clock, and started on Rollins.

The sound of Wolfe's elevator came, and he appeared, told me good morning, crossed to his chair and got his poundage adjusted, and spoke. "I left my papers in my room. May I have yours?"

I should have put them on his desk, since I knew he had had company for breakfast. I took them to him and then resumed at the typewriter. He glanced through the morning mail, which was mostly circulars and requests from worthy causes, then settled back with the news. That was okay, since there could have been an item that might affect the program for the day. He is not a fast reader, and I pounded along in high so as to be finished by the time he was ready. It was still before noon by ten minutes when I rolled the last page of Rollins from the machine, and after collating the originals and carbons I turned for a glance at him.

He had put the papers down and was deep in *Beauty for Ashes.*

No commonplace crack would fit the situation. It was serious and could be critical. I stapled the reports, labeled a folder "Lippert, Buff and Assa" and put them in it, went and put the folder in the cabinet, came back to my desk and put things away, turned to him and announced, "I'm all set. Hansen and Buff phoned to ask how we're coming, and I told them there was no use crowding. Philip Younger wants you to get him a conference with LBA, and I said maybe later. Lon Cohen wants the murderer's name with a picture by five o'clock. That's the crop. I'm ready for instructions."

He finished a paragraph—no, it was verse. He finished something, then his eyes came at me over the top of the book. "I haven't any," he stated.

"Oh. Tomorrow, maybe? Or some day next week?"

"I don't know. I gave it some thought last night, and I don't know."

I stared at him. "This is your finest hour," I said emphatically. "This is the rawest you have ever pulled. You took the case just twenty-four hours ago. Why didn't you turn it down? That you have the gall to sit there on your fanny and read poetry is bad enough, but that you tell me to do likewise . . ." I stood up. "I quit."

"I haven't told you to read poetry."

"You might as well. I'm quitting, and I'm going to the ball game."

He shook his head. "You can't quit in the middle of a case, and you can't go to the ball game because I couldn't get you if you were suddenly needed."

"Needed for what? Bring you beer?"

"No." He put the book down, drew a long deep sigh, and leaned back. "I suppose this has to be. You're enraged because I haven't devised a list of sallies and exploits for you. You have of course pondered the situation, as I have. I sympathize with your eagerness to do something. What would you suggest?"

"It's not up to me. If I did the suggesting around here, that would be my desk and this would be yours."

"Nevertheless, I put it to you. Please sit down so I can look at you without stretching my neck. Thank you. There is nothing you can do about any of these people that the police have not already done, and are doing, with incomparably greater resources and numbers. Keeping them under surveillance, investigating their past, learning if any of them had a gun, checking their alibis, harassing them by prolonged and repetitive inquisition—do you want to compete with the police on any of those?"

"You know damn well I don't. I want you to go to work and come up with instructions for me. Unless Saul is handling it?"

"Saul has been given a little task I didn't want to spare you for. You will accept my decision that at the moment there is nothing to be done by either you or me. That condition may continue for a week, until after the deadline has come and gone. Messrs. Hansen and Buff and O'Garro and Assa—and Mr. Heery too—are quite wrong in thinking that the culprit must be exposed before the deadline; on the contrary, it will be much more feasible after the deadline, unless—"

"That won't do us any good. You can't stall them that long. They'll bounce you."

"I doubt it. I'd have something to say about it. And anyway, I was saying that it will be more feasible after the deadline unless something happens, and I rather think that something will. The tension is extremely severe, not only for the culprit, but also for the others, in one way or another. That's why you can't go to the ball game; you must be at hand. Also for the phone calls. They'll get increasingly exigent and must be handled discreetly but firmly. I could help some with them, but it would be best for me to be so deeply engaged with the problem that I am unavailable. Of course they are not to be told that I think the solution may have to wait until after the deadline."

"Say by the Fourth of July," I suggested bitterly.

"Sooner than that or not at all." He was tolerant. "Commonly I take your badgering as a necessary evil; it has on occasion served a purpose; but this may go on for a while and I wish to be spared. I assure you, Archie—"

The phone rang. I answered it, and a trained female voice told me that Mr. O'Garro wanted to speak with Mr. Wolfe. Evidently they were reverting to type up at LBA. I told her Mr. Wolfe was engaged, but Mr. O'Garro could speak with Mr. Goodwin if he cared to. She said he wanted Mr. Wolfe, and I said I was sorry he couldn't have him. She told me to hold on, and after a wait resumed by asking me to put Mr. Goodwin on, and I said he was on. Then I got a male voice: "Hello, Goodwin? This is Pat O'Garro. I want to speak to Wolfe!"

"So I understand, but I have strict instructions not to disturb him, and I don't dare to. When he's buried in a case, as he is right now in yours, it's not only bad for me if I interrupt him, it's bad for the case. You've given him a tough one to crack, and you'd better leave him alone with it."

"My God, we've got to know what he's doing!"

"No, sir. Excuse me, but you're dead wrong. You either rely on him to get it or you don't. When he's working as hard as he is on this he never tells anybody what he's doing, and it's a big mistake to ask him. As soon as there's anything you'd like to know or need to know or can help with, you'll hear without delay. I told Mr. Hansen, and also Mr. Buff, about Inspector Cramer calling on us last night."

"I know you did. What time this afternoon can I drop in?"

"Any time that suits you. I'll be here, and you can look at the transcripts of the talks with the contestants if you want to. Mr. Wolfe will be upstairs and not available. When he's sunk in a thing as he is in this it's a job to get him to eat."

"But damn it, what's he doing?"

"He's using the brain you hired. Didn't you gentlemen decide you needed a special kind of brain? All right, you got one."

"We certainly did. I'll see you this afternoon."

I told him that would be fine, and hung up, and turned to ask Wolfe if that would do, but he had lifted his book and opened it and I didn't want to disturb him.

12

Thank the Lord those next four days are behind me instead of ahead. I admit that there are operations and situations where the best you can do is set a trap and then wait patiently for the victim to spring it, and in such a case I can wait as patiently as the next one, but we had set no trap. Waiting for the victim to make the trap himself and then spring it called for more patience than I had in stock.

Wolfe had asked me what I would suggest, and I spent part of the time from Thursday noon to Friday noon, in between phone calls and personal appearances of LBA personnel and Talbott Heery, trying to hit on something. I had to agree with him that there was no point in tagging along after the cops on any of the routines. Altogether, while sitting at my desk or on the stool in the kitchen, or brushing my teeth, or shaving, or looking out the window, I conceived at least a dozen bright ideas, none of them worth a damn when you turned them over. I did submit one of them to Wolfe after dinner Thursday evening: to get the five contestants together in the office, and tell them it had been thought that Dahlmann had put the answers to the last five verses in a safe deposit box, but evidently he hadn't, since none could be found, and there was no authentic list of answers against which their solutions could be checked, and therefore other verses, not yet devised, would have to replace the ones they had. He asked what good it would do. I said we would get their reactions. He said we already had their reactions, and besides, LBA would properly reject a procedure that made them out a bunch of bungling boobies.

There was nothing in Friday's papers that struck a spark, but at least they didn't announce that Cramer had got his man and the case was solved. Just the contrary. No one had been tapped even as a material witness, and it was plain, from the way the *Gazette* handled it, that the field was still wide open. Lon Cohen phoned again around noon to ask what Wolfe was waiting for, and I told him for a flash. He asked what kind of flash, and I told him to ask Miss Frazee.

The climax of the phone calls from the clients began soon after lunch Friday. Wolfe was up in his room to be away from the turmoil. He had finished *Beauty for Ashes* and started on *Party of One*, not in verse, by Clifton Fadiman. The climax was in three scenes, the hero of the first one being Patrick O'Garro. It was the third call from him in the twenty-four hours, and he made it short and to the point. He asked to speak to Wolfe and I gave him the usual dose. He asked if I had anything to report and I said no.

"All right," he said, "that's enough. This is formal notice that our agreement with him is canceled and he is no longer representing Lippert, Buff and Assa. This conversation is being recorded. He can send a bill for services to date. Did you hear me?"

"Sure I hear you. I'd like to say more because my phone conversations don't get recorded very often, but there's nothing to say. Goodbye."

I went to the hall, up the flight of stairs to Wolfe's room, tapped on the door, and entered. He was in the big chair by the window, in his shirt sleeves with his vest unbuttoned, with his book.

"You look nice and comfortable," I said approvingly, "but you prefer the chair downstairs and you can come on down if you want to. O'Garro just phoned and canceled the order. We're fired. He said the conversation was being recorded. I wonder why it makes a man feel important to have what he says on the phone recorded? I don't mean him, I mean me."

"Bosh," he said.

"No, really, it *did* make me feel important."

"Shut up." He closed his eyes. In a minute he opened them. "Very well. I'll be down shortly. It's a confounded nuisance."

I agreed and left him. As I went back downstairs my feelings were mixed. Getting tossed out on our ear would certainly be no fun, it wouldn't help our prestige any, and it would reduce our bill by about ninety-five per cent to a mere exorbitant charge for consultation, but I did not burst into tears as I began strolling around the office to wait for developments. At least the fat son of a gun would have to snap out of it and show something. At least his eyes would get a rest from the strain of constant reading. At least I wouldn't have to try to dig up more ways of explaining why they couldn't speak to a genius while he was fermenting.

The phone rang, and I answered it, and was told by a baritone that I recognized, "This is Rudolph Hansen. I want to speak to Mr. Wolfe."

I didn't bother. I said curtly, "Nothing doing. Orders not to disturb."

"Nonsense. He has already been disturbed by the message from Mr. O'Garro. Let me speak to him."

"I haven't given him the message from O'Garro. When he tells me to disturb him on no account he means it."

"You haven't given him that message?"

"No, sir."

"Why not?"

"My God, how many times must I say it? Do . . . not . . . disturb."

"That certainly is a strange way of—no matter. It's just as well. Mr. O'Garro was too impetuous. His message is hereby canceled, on my authority as counsel for the firm of Lippert, Buff and Assa. Mr. Wolfe is too highhanded and we would like to be kept better informed, but we have full confidence in him and we want him to go on. Tell him that—no, I'll tell him. I'll drop in a little later. I'm tied up here for the present."

I thanked him for calling, hung up, and mounted the stairs again to Wolfe's room; and by gum, he wasn't reading. He had put the book down and was sitting there looking imposed upon.

"I said I'd be down shortly," he growled.

"Yeah, but you don't have to. Go right on working. Hansen phoned as counsel for the firm. O'Garro was too impetuous, he said. They have full confidence in you, which shows how little—oh well. You're to keep at it. I didn't ask him if the conversation was recorded."

He picked up his book. "Very well. Now you may reasonably expect a respite."

"Not for long. Hansen's dropping in later."

He grunted and I left him.

The respite was a good ten minutes, maybe eleven, and it was ended at the worst possible moment. I had turned on the television and got the ball game, Giants and Dodgers, and Willie Mays was at bat in the fourth inning with a count of two and one, when the phone rang. Dialing the sound off but not the picture, I got at the phone, and received a double jolt. With my ears I heard Oliver Buff saying that both O'Garro and Hansen were too impetuous and had it wrong, and going on from there, and simultaneously with my eyes I saw Mays pop a soft blooper into short center field that I could have caught on the tip of my nose. I turned my back on that, but the rest of Buff I had to take. When he was through I went and turned off the TV, and once again ascended the stairs.

Wolfe frowned at me suspiciously. "Is this flummery?" he demanded.

"Not to my knowledge," I told him. "It sounds like their voices."

"Pfui. I mean you. The call by Mr. Hansen voided the one by Mr. O'Garro. You could have invented both of them; it would be typical."

"Sure I could, but I didn't. You asked for a cease-fire on badgering and got it. This time it was Buff. LBA seems to be tossing coins and giving me a play-by-play report. Buff voided both O'Garro and Hansen. He says they have been conferring and just reached a decision. They want a report by you personally on progress to date, and they're all at the LBA office, including Talbott Heery, and can't leave to come here, so you're to go there. At once. Otherwise the deal is off. I told him, first, that you never go outdoors on business, and second, that I wasn't supposed to disturb you and I wasn't going to. He had heard that before. He said you would be there by four o'clock, or else. It is now a quarter past three. May I offer a suggestion?"

"What?"

"If you ever take another job for that outfit, even to find out who's stealing the paper clips, get it in writing, signed by everybody. I'm tired out running up and down stairs."

He didn't hear me. With his elbow on the chair arm, he was pulling gently at the tip of his nose with thumb and forefinger. After a little he spoke. "As I said yesterday, the tension is extremely severe, and something had to snap. I doubt if this is it. This is probably merely the froth of frustration, but it may be suggestive to watch the bubbles. How long will it take you to get there?"

"This time of day, fifteen to twenty minutes."

"Ample. Get them together. All of them."

"Sure. Do I just tell them I'm you, or shall I borrow one of your suits and some pillows?"

"You are yourself, Archie. But I must define your posi-

80

tion. You've been demanding instructions and here they
are. Sit down."

I moved a chair up.

13

My visit to their office that afternoon probably cost
LBA around three grand, maybe even five, for I
found occasion later to describe the layout to Wolfe, thinking he should have it in mind when he was deciding on
the amount of his bill, which he surely did if I know him.

From the directory in the lobby of the modern midtown
skyscraper I learned that LBA had six floors, which
opened my eyes and made me pick one. Choosing twenty-
two because it was marked *Executive,* I found the proper
elevator, was lifted, and emerged into a chamber that
would have been fine for badminton if you took up the
rugs. With upholstered chairs here and there sort of care-
lessly, and spots of light from modern lamps, it was a very
cultured atmosphere. Two or three of the chairs were
occupied, and at the far side, facing the elevators, an
aristocratic brunette with nice little ears was seated at an
executive desk eight feet long. When I approached she
asked if she could help me, and I told her my name and
said I wanted to see Mr. Buff.

"Do you have an appointment, Mr. Goodwin?"

"Yes, but under an alias, Nero Wolfe."

That only confused her and made her suspicious, but I
finally got it straightened out and she used the phone and
asked me to wait. I was crossing to a chair when a door
opened and Vernon Assa appeared. He stood a moment,
wiping his brow and neck with a handkerchief, and then
came to me. Short plump men are inclined to sweat, but
it did seem that an LBA top executive might have finished
wiping before entering the reception room.

"Where's Mr. Wolfe?" he asked.

"At home. I'll report. To all of you."

"I don't think—" He hesitated. "Come with me."

We passed through into a wide carpeted hall. The third door on the left was standing open and we turned in. It was a fairly large room and would be a handsome one after the cleaning women had been around, but at present it was messy. The gleaming top of the big mahogany table in the center had most of its gleam spotted with cigarette ashes and stray pieces of paper, and the nine or ten executive-size chairs were every which way. A cigar butt had spilled out of an ash tray onto the mahogany.

Three men, not counting Assa, looked at me, and I looked at them. Talbott Heery wasn't so broad and tall when he had slid so far forward in his chair that most of him was underneath the table. Buff's white hair was tousled, and his round red face was puffy. He was seated across from Heery and had to twist around to look at me. Rudolph Hansen's long thin neck had a big smudge below the right ear. He was standing to one side with his arms folded and his narrow shoulders slumped.

"Goodwin says he'll report," Assa told them. "We can hear what he has to say."

"To all of you," I said, not aggressively. "Including Mr. O'Garro."

"He's in a meeting and can't be here."

"Then I'll wait." I sat down. "He canceled the agreement, and it wouldn't do much good to come to an understanding with you if he phones as soon as I get back and cancels it."

"That was on his own initiative," Buff said, "and unauthorized."

"Isn't he a member of the firm?"

"Yes."

"Okay. I'll wait. If I'm in the way here, tell me where."

"Get him in here," Heery demanded. "He can get the goddam toothpaste account any time."

They all started clawing, not at me but at each other. I sat and watched the bubbles, and heard them. LBA was certainly boiling over, and I tried to take it in, knowing that Wolfe would want a verbatim report, but it got a little confused. Finally they got it decided, I didn't know exactly how, and Buff got at a phone and talked, and pretty soon the door opened and Patrick O'Garro was with us. He was still brown all over, and his quick brown eyes were blazing.

"Are you all feeble-minded?" he blurted. "I said I'd go along with whatever you decided. I don't intend—"

I cut in. "Hold it, Mr. O'Garro. It's my fault. I came to report for Mr. Wolfe, and you have got to be present. I'm willing to wait, but they're in a hurry—some of them."

He said something cutting to Heery, and the others chimed in, and I thought the boiling was going to start again, but Buff got up and took O'Garro's arm and eased him to a chair. Then Buff returned to his own chair, which was next to me at the left.

"All right, Goodwin," he said. "Go ahead."

I took a paper from my pocket and unfolded it. "First," I announced, "here is a letter to Mr. Hansen, signed by Mr. Wolfe. It's only one sentence. It says, 'I herewith dismiss you as my attorney and instruct you not to represent me in any matter whatsoever.' Mr. Wolfe told me to deliver it before witnesses." I handed it to Assa, he handed it to O'Garro, and he handed it to Hansen. Hansen glanced at it, folded it, and put it in his pocket.

"Proceed," he said stiffly.

"Yes, sir. There are three points to consider. The first is the job itself and how you people have handled it. In the years I have been with Mr. Wolfe he has had a lot of damn fools for clients, but you have come pretty close to the record. Apparently you—"

"For God's sake," O'Garro demanded, "do you call that reporting? We want to know what he's done!"

"Well, you're not going to. Apparently you haven't stopped to realize what the job's like. I'll put it this way: if he knew right now who went there and stole the wallet —and killed Dahlmann, put that in too—and all he needed was one additional piece of evidence and he knew he was going to get it tonight—if he knew all that, he wouldn't tell any of you one single damn thing about it. Not before he had it absolutely sewed up. In the condition of panic you're in, all of you except Mr. Hansen, I don't know how much you can understand, but maybe you can understand that."

"I can't," Buff said. "It sounds preposterous. We hired him and we'll pay him."

"Then I'll spell it out. What would happen if he kept you posted on exactly what he had done and was doing and intended to do? God only knows, but judging from the way you've been acting this afternoon there would be a riot. One or another of you would be calling every ten minutes to cancel what the last one said and give him new instructions. Mr. Wolfe doesn't take instructions, he takes a job, and you should have known that before you hired him. —You did, didn't you, Mr. Hansen? You said that all of you would be at his mercy."

"Not precisely in that sense." The lawyer's eyes, meeting mine, were cold and steady. "But I knew of Wolfe's methods and manners, yes. I grant that the conflicting messages from us this afternoon were ill-advised, but we are under great pressure. We need to know at least whether any progress is being made."

"You will, when he is ready to tell you. He's under pressure too. You have to consider that he's not working for you . . . or you . . . or you . . . or you . . . or you. He's working for the firm of Lippert, Buff and Assa. I can say this, if the men authorized to speak for the firm want to call it off, it may be possible to make another arrangement. Just a suggestion: do you want to ask Mr. Heery if he cares to take over and have Mr. Wolfe represent him instead of LBA?"

"No!" O'Garro blurted. Assa looked at Hansen and the lawyer shook his head. Buff said, "I can't see that that would improve the situation any. Our interests are identical." Heery, sending his eyes around, said, "If you want it that way, say so."

Nobody said so. I gave them four seconds and went on. "Another point. I've told you that Inspector Cramer of Homicide came to see Mr. Wolfe last night. I'm not quoting him, but when he left Mr. Wolfe's main impression was that he wasn't completely sold on the idea that one of the contestants killed Dahlmann to get the paper in the wallet. Someone could have killed him for a quite different reason and didn't take the wallet or anything else, and later one of you went there to see him and found him dead. You looked to see if the wallet was in his pocket, and it was, and you didn't want it found on his body on account of the risk that what was on the paper might possibly be made public, so you took the wallet and beat it. That would—"

They all broke in. Hansen said, "Absurd. Mr. Wolfe certainly wasn't—"

"Just a minute," I stopped him. "Mr. Wolfe told Cramer that he thought it likely that one of the contestants took the wallet, and that he was assuming that whoever killed Dahlmann took the wallet, but that doesn't mean he can toss Cramer's idea in the garbage as a pipe dream. He has no proof it didn't happen like that; all he has is what you men told him. So if he doesn't want to run the risk of being made a monkey of, which he doesn't, believe me, he has to keep that on the list of possibles, and in that case how can he tell you what he's doing and going to do? Tell who? His client is Lippert, Buff and Assa, but there's no such person as Lippert, Buff and Assa, it would have to be one of you, and it might be the very guy who went to Dahlmann's place and retrieved the wallet. Therefore——"

"It's absurd on the face of it," Hansen said. "It would——"

"Let me finish. Therefore Mr. Wolfe has a double reason not to keep you posted on every move—first, he never does with anybody, and second, one of you could be holding out on him and set to spike him. I don't think he thinks you are, but it's a cinch he wouldn't take that chance. There's no use trying to persuade me it's absurd, because Mr. Wolfe is the expert on absurdity, not me, and I wouldn't undertake to pass it on. That about covers the situation, except this, that he's fed up with your shoving. I had to disturb him to tell him about the performance you have put on this afternoon because I had to ask him if he wanted me to come up here, and I am now reporting that he is fed up. He is willing to go on with the job only with the understanding that what he is committed to get for you is results as they were outlined, as quickly and satisfactorily as possible, using his best ability and judgment. If you want him to continue on that basis, okay. If not, he might be willing to take on the job for Mr. Heery, but I doubt it, without the consent and approval of LBA, because you're all in it together."

"What then?" Hansen asked, colder than ever. "He has dismissed me as his attorney. What would he do?"

"I don't know, but I can give you a guess, and I know him fairly well. I think he would give Inspector Cramer the whole story as he knows it, including whatever he may have learned since he talked with you people, and forget it."

"Let him!" O'Garro barked. "To hell with him!"

Buff said, "Take it easy, Pat."

"I think we're overlooking something," Assa said. "We've let our personal feelings get involved, and that's wrong. The one thing we all want is to save the contest, and what we've got to ask ourselves is whether we're more likely to do that with Wolfe or without him. Let me ask you this, Goodwin. I agree with Mr. Hansen that Inspector Cramer's idea is absurd, but just suppose that Wolfe did find evidence, or thought he did, that one of us went to Dahlmann's apartment and found him dead and took the wallet. Whom would he report it to?"

"That would depend. If LBA was still his client, to LBA. He was hired—these were Hansen's words—*to find out who took the wallet and got the paper*. If he did what he was hired to do, or thought he had, naturally he would tell his client and no one else. There would be two offenses involved, swiping a wallet and failing to report discovery of a dead body, but that wouldn't bother him. But he couldn't report to a client if he no longer had one, and my guess is he would just empty the bag for Cramer."

"That," Hansen said, "is an unmistakable threat."

"Is it?" I grinned at him. "That's bad. I thought I was just answering a question. I withdraw it."

Talbott Heery, across the mahogany top from me, suddenly was up and on his feet, in all his height and breadth, glaring around with no favorites. "If I ever saw a bunch of lightweights," he told them, "this is it. You know goddam well Nero Wolfe is our only hope of getting out of this without losing most of our hide, and listen to you!" He put two fists on the table. "I'll tell you this right now: at the end of the contract you're done with Heery Products! If I had had any sense—"

"Tape it, Tal." O'Garro's voice was raised, with a sneer in it. "Go downstairs and tape it! We'll get along without you and without Nero Wolfe too! I don't—"

The others joined in and they were boiling again. I was perfectly willing to sit and watch the bubbles, but Oliver Buff arose and took my sleeve and practically pulled me to my feet, and was steering me to the door. His teeth were set on his lower lip, but had to release it for speech. "If you'll wait outside," he said, pushing me into the hall. "We'll send for you." He shut the door.

Outside could have meant right there, but eavesdropping is vulgar if you can't distinguish words, and I soon found that I couldn't, so I moseyed down the wide carpeted hall and on through into the reception room. A couple of the upholstered chairs had customers, but not the same ones as when I had arrived. When I lingered instead of pushing the elevator button the aristocratic brunette at the desk gave me a look, and, not wanting her to worry, I went and told her the evidence was all in and I was waiting for the verdict. She had a notion to give me a smile—I was wearing a dark brown pin-stripe that was a good fit, with a solid tan shirt and a soft wool medium-brown tie—but decided it would be better to wait until we heard the verdict. I decided she was too cagey for one of my temperament, and crossed the rugs over to a battery of large cabinets with glass fronts that covered all of a wall and part of two others. They were filled with an assortment of objects of all sizes, shapes, colors, and materials.

Being a detective, I soon detected what they were: samples of the products of LBA clients, past and present. I thought it was very democratic to have them here in the executive reception room instead of down on a lower floor with the riffraff. Altogether there must have been several thousand different items, from spark plugs to ocean liners to paper drinking cups to pharmaceuticals—though in the case of the liners and trucks and refrigerators, and other bulky items, they had settled for photographs instead of the real thing. There was an elegant little model of a completely equipped super-modern kitchen, about eighteen inches long, that I would have taken home for a doll's house, if I had had a wife and we had had a child and the child had been a girl and the girl had liked dolls. I was having a second look at the Heery Products section, which alone had over a hundred specimens, and was trying to decide what I thought of yellow for packaging, when the brunette called my name and I turned.

"You may go in," she said, and darned if the smile didn't nearly break through. Of course she had had plenty of time to inspect me from behind, and I never had a suit that fitted better. I repaid her with a friendly glance that spoke volumes as I stepped to the door to the inner hall.

In the executive committee room, I suppose it was, I couldn't tell from their expressions who or what had won. Certainly nobody looked happy or even hopeful. Heery was at a window with his back to us, which I thought was tactful since technically he was not a party. The others eyed me without love as I approached the big table.

Hansen spoke. "We have decided to have Nero Wolfe continue with the case, using his best ability and judgment as you stated, without prejudice to any of our rights and privileges. Including the right to be informed on matters affecting our interests, but leaving that to his discretion for the present."

I had my notebook out and was jotting it down. That done, I asked, "Unanimous? Mr. Wolfe will want to know. Do you concur, Mr. Buff?"

"Yes," he said firmly.

"Mr. Assa?"

"Yes," he said wearily.

"Mr. O'Garro?"

"Yes," he said rudely.

"Good." I returned the notebook to my pocket. "I'll do my best to persuade Mr. Wolfe to carry on, and if you don't hear from me within an hour you'll know it's okay. I'd like to add one little point: as his confidential assistant I'm in it too somewhat, and it interferes with my chores to spend half my time answering your phone calls, so I personally request you to keep your shirts on."

I turned to go, but Buff caught my sleeve. "You understand, Goodwin, that the time element is vital. Only five days. And we hope Wolfe understands it."

"Sure he does. Before midnight Wednesday. That's why he can't bear to be disturbed."

I left them to their misery. Passing through the reception room I paused to tell the brunette, "Guilty on all counts. See you up the river." It was a shock for her.

14

The next two days, Saturday and Sunday, I found that my personal request had been a mistake. Thursday and Friday had been bad enough, but at least their phone calls had given me something to do now and then, and with them muzzled, or nearly so, my patience got a tougher test than ever. You might think that after putting up with Wolfe for so long I would be acclimatized, and I am up to a point, but he keeps breaking records. After I reported to him in full on my session at LBA, including a description of the premises, there was practically no mention of the case for more than sixty hours. By Monday morning I was willing to believe he had really meant it when he said it would be more feasible after the deadline, and I had to admit that at least it was an original idea to use a deadline for a starting barrier.

I spent most of the weekend prowling around the house, but was allowed to go out occasionally to walk myself around the block, and even made a couple of calls. Saturday afternoon I dropped in at Manhattan Homicide West on Twentieth Street for a little visit with Sergeant Purley Stebbins. Naturally he was suspicious, thinking that Wolfe had sent me to pry something loose, if only a desk and a couple of chairs, but he also thought I might have something to peddle, so we chatted a while. When I got up to go he actually said there was no hurry. Later, back home, when I reported to Wolfe and told him I was offering twenty to one that the cops were as cold as we were, his only comment was an indifferent grunt.

Late Sunday afternoon I spent six bucks of LBA money buying drinks for Lon Cohen at Yaden's bar. I told him I wanted the total lowdown on all aspects of the Dahlmann case, and he offered to autograph a copy of yesterday's *Gazette* for me. He was a great help. Among the items of unprinted scuttlebutt were these: Dahlmann had welshed on a ninety-thousand-dollar poker debt. His wallet had contained an assortment of snapshots of society women, undressed. He had double-crossed a prominent politician on a publicity deal. All the members of his firm had hated his guts and ganged up on him. The name of one of the several dozen women he had played games with was Ellen Heery, the wife of Talbott. He had been a Russian spy. He had got something on a certain philanthropist and been blackmailing him. And so on. The usual crop, Lon said, with a few fancy touches as tributes to Dahlmann's outstanding personality. Lon would of course not believe that Wolfe wasn't working on the murder, and almost refused to accept another drink when he was convinced that I had no handout for him.

I gave Wolfe the scuttlebutt, but apparently he wasn't listening. It was Sunday evening, when he especially enjoys turning the television off. Of course he has to turn it on first, intermittently throughout the evening, and that takes a lot of exertion, but he has provided for it by installing a remote control panel at his desk. That way he can turn off as many as twenty programs in an evening without overdoing. Ordinarily I am not there, since I spend most of my Sunday evenings trying to give pleasure to some fellow being, no matter who she is provided she meets certain specifications, but that Sunday I stuck around. If something did snap on account of the extremely severe tension, as Wolfe had claimed he thought it might, I was going to be there. When I went up to bed, early, he was turning off *Silver Linings*.

The snap, if that's the right word for it, came a little after ten o'clock Monday morning, in the shape of a phone call, not for Wolfe but for me.

"You don't sound like Archie Goodwin," a male voice said.

"Well, I am. You do sound like Philip Younger."

"I ought to. You're Goodwin?"

"Yes. The one who turned down your Scotch."

"That sounds better. I want to see you right away. I'm in my room at the Churchill. Get here as fast as you can."

"Coming. Hold everything."

That shows the condition I was in. I should have asked him what was up. I should at least have learned if a gun was being leveled at him. Speaking of guns, I should have followed my rule to take one along. But I was so damn sick and tired of nothing I was in favor of anything, and quick. I dived into the kitchen to tell Fritz to tell Wolfe where I was going, grabbed my hat and coat as I passed the rack, ran down the stoop steps, and hoofed it double quick to Tenth Avenue for a taxi, through the scattered drops of the beginning of an April shower.

As we were crawling uptown with the thousand-wheeled worm I muttered to the hackie, "Try the sidewalk."

"It's only Monday," he said gloomily. "Got a whole week."

We finally made it to the Churchill, and I went in and took an elevator, ignored the floor clerk on the eighteenth, went to the door of eighteen-twenty-six, knocked, and was told to come in. Younger, looking a little less like Old King Cole when up and dressed, wanted to shake hands and I had no objection.

"It took you long enough," he complained. "I know, I know, I live in Chicago. Sit down. I want to ask you something."

I thought, my God, all for nothing, he's got another idea about splitting the pot and yanked me up here to sell it. I took a chair and he sat on the edge of the bed, which hadn't been made.

"I just got something in the mail," he said, "and I'm not sure what to do with it. I could give it to the police, but I don't want to. The ones I've seen haven't impressed me. Do you know a Lieutenant Rowcliff?"

"I sure do. You can have him."

"I don't want him. Then there's those advertising men with Dahlmann at that meeting, that's where I met them, but I've seen them since, and they don't impress me either. I was going to phone a man I know in Chicago, a lawyer, but it would take a lot of explaining on the phone, the whole mess. So I thought of you. You know all about it, and when you were here the other day I offered you a drink. When I offer a man a drink without thinking, that's a good sign. I can go by that as well as anything. I've got to do something about this and do it quick, and the first thing is to show it to you and see what you say."

He took an envelope from his pocket, looked at it, looked at me, and handed it over. I inspected the envelope of ordinary cheap white paper, which had jagged edges where it had been torn open. Typewritten address to Mr. Philip Younger, Churchill Hotel. No return address front or back. Three-cent stamp, postmarked Grand Central Station 11:00 PM APR 17 1955. It contained a single sheet of folded paper, and I took it out and unfolded it. It was medium-grade sulphide bond, with nothing printed on it, but with plenty of something typewritten. It was headed at the top in caps: ANSWERS TO THE FIVE VERSES DISTRIBUTED ON APRIL 12TH. Below were the names of five women, with a brief commentary on each. I kept my face deadpan as I ran over them and saw that they were the real McCoy.

"Well," I said, "this is interesting. What is it, a gag?"

"That's the trouble—or one trouble. I'm not sure. I think it's the real answers, but I don't know. I'd have to go to a library and check. I was going to, and then I thought this is dynamite, and I thought of you. Isn't that the first—hey, I want that! That's mine!"

I had absent-mindedly folded the paper and put it in the envelope and was sticking it in my pocket. "Sure," I said, "take it." He took it. "It's somewhat of a problem. Let me think." I sat and thought a minute. "It looks to me," I said, "that you're probably right, the first thing to do is to check it. But the police are probably still tailing all of you. Have you been going to libraries the last few days?"

"No. I decided not to. I don't know my way around in any library here, and those two women, Frazee and Tescher, have got too big an advantage. I decided to fight it instead."

I nodded sympathetically. "Then if a cop tails you to a library now, only two days to the deadline, they'll wonder why you started in all of a sudden, and they'll want to know. The man I work for, Nero Wolfe, is quite a reader and he has quite a library. I noticed the titles of the books mentioned on that thing, and I wouldn't be surprised if he has all of them. Also it wouldn't hurt any for you to consult him about this."

"I'm consulting you."

"Yeah, but I haven't got the library with me. And if a cop tails you to his place it won't matter. They know he's representing Lippert, Buff and Assa about the contest, and all the contestants have been there except you."

"That's what I don't like. He's representing them and I'm fighting them."

"Then you shouldn't have showed it to me. I work for Mr. Wolfe, and if you think I won't tell him about it you'll have to take back what you said the other day about not making a fool of yourself for twenty-six years. Crap."

He looked pleased. "See," he said, "you remembered that."

"I remember everything. So the choice is merely whether I tell Mr. Wolfe or you tell him, and if you do you can use his library."

He was no wobbler. He went and opened a closet door and got out a hat and topcoat. As he was putting an arm in he said, "I don't suppose you drink in the morning."

"No, thanks." I was headed for the door. "But if you want one go ahead."

"I quit twenty-six years ago." He motioned for me to precede him, followed, pulled the door shut, and tried it to make sure it was locked. "But," he added, "now that I can afford little luxuries, thanks to my son-in-law, I like to have some around for other people." As we turned the corner of the hall he finished, *"Some* other people." On the way down in the elevator it occurred to me that he would want the verses to refer to, and I asked if he had them with him, and he said yes.

To make sure whether your taxi is being followed in midtown traffic takes a lot of maneuvering, which takes time, and Younger and I decided we didn't really give a damn, so except for a few backward glances out of curiosity we skipped it. At the curb in front of the old brownstone on West Thirty-fifth I paid the driver, got out, led the way up the steps to the stoop, and pushed the button. In a moment the door was opened by Fritz, who, as I was taking Younger's coat, made sure I saw his extended forefinger, meaning that a visitor was in the office with Wolfe. Acknowledging it with a nod, I ushered Younger across the hall into the front room, told him it would be a short wait, and, instead of using the connecting door to the office, which was soundproofed, went around by way of the hall.

Wolfe was in his chair, with half a dozen books in front of him on his desk, but he wasn't reading. He was frowning at Mrs. James R. Wheelock of Richmond, Virginia, who was in the red leather chair, frowning back at him. The frowns switched to me as I approached. I was a little slow meeting them because it took me a second to get the title of the book on top of the pile: *The Letters of Dorothy Osborne to Sir William Temple.* With that, which was enough, I told Mrs. Wheelock good morning, informed Wolfe that Fritz wanted him in the kitchen for something, and walked out.

When he joined me in the kitchen the frown was gone and there was a gleam in his eye. I spoke first. "I just wanted to ask you if she has any idea who mailed her the answers."

It got him for half a second. Then he said, "Oh. Mr. Younger got them too?"

"He did. That's what he wanted to see me about. He's in the front room. He wanted to find out if the answers are the real thing, and I told him he could use your library, but I see Mrs. Wheelock had the same idea."

"No. She merely wished to tell me, and consult me. I suggested looking at the books; luckily I had all of them. I hadn't hoped for anything as provocative as this. Very satisfactory."

"Yeah. Worth waiting for. A slight comedown for me, to bring home a slab of bacon and find you're already slicing one just like it, but anyhow we've got it. Shall I send mine back?"

"By no means." He pursed his lips, and in a moment continued, "I'll tell her. You tell him. Bring him in in three minutes." He was gone.

I returned to the front room and found Younger on a chair by a window with a sheet of paper in each hand, one presumably being the verses. "You're not the only one," I told him. "Mrs. Wheelock got it too, and came to show it to Mr. Wolfe. She's in there with him now. He has the books, and they've checked the answers, and it's not a gag."

He squinted at me. "She got—just like this?"

"I haven't seen it, but of course it is."

"And they've checked it?"

"Right."

He stood up. "I want to see hers. Where is she?"

"You will." I looked at my wrist. "In one minute and twenty seconds."

"I'll be damned. Then it's not a frame. That was one thing I thought, that someone was trying to frame me, but I couldn't see how. She got it in the mail this morning?"

I told him she would no doubt be glad to supply all details, and right at the deadline crossed to open the door to the office and invited him in. He brushed on by, went straight to Mrs. Wheelock, and demanded, "Where's the one you got?"

I went and took his elbow, called his attention to Wolfe, steered him to a chair, and told Wolfe, "Mr. Younger wants details. Is hers like his and when did she get it and so on."

Wolfe lifted a sheet of paper from his desk blotter. Younger popped up from his chair and went to him. I joined them, and so did Mrs. Wheelock. It didn't take much comparing to see that hers was a carbon copy of his. The envelopes, including the postmarks, were the same except for the names. When Younger had satisfied himself on those points he picked up one of the books, Casanova's *Memoirs*, and opened it. Mrs. Wheelock told him that wasn't necessary, they were the right answers, no question about it. She didn't look as if she had changed her attitude to the food at the Churchill, but the fire back of her dark deep-set eyes was shining through in her excitement. Younger went ahead anyway, finding a page in the book, and we were still grouped at Wolfe's desk when the phone rang.

I went to my desk to answer it, and got from the receiver the same old refrain. "I want to speak to Mr. Wolfe. This is Talbott Heery."

But the lid was off, maybe. I told Wolfe, and he took his instrument, and I kept mine.

"This is Nero Wolfe. Yes, Mr. Heery?"

"I'm calling from my office. Harold Rollins, one of the contestants, is here. He just came, a few minutes ago, to show me something he received in the mail this morning. I have it here in my hand. It's a typewritten sheet of paper, headed, 'Answers to the five verses distributed on April twelfth,' and then the names of five women and comments on each. Of course I don't know whether they are the correct answers or not, but Rollins says they are. He says he came to me because this nullifies the contest, and my company is responsible. I'll consult my lawyer on

95

that—not Rudolph Hansen—but I'm calling you first. What have you got to say?"

"Not much offhand. Mr. Rollins is with you?"

"He's in my office. I came to another room to phone. By God, this does it. Now what?"

"That needs a little thought. You may tell Mr. Rollins that he was not singled out. Mrs. Wheelock and Mr. Younger also received sheets in the mail like the one you describe. They are here on my desk—that is, the sheets are. Mrs. Wheelock and Mr. Younger are here with me. Probably all five—"

"We've got to do something! We've got—"

"Please, Mr. Heery." For years I have studied Wolfe's trick of stopping a man without raising his voice, but I still don't get it. "Something must indeed be done, I agree, but this doesn't heighten the urgency. Rather the contrary. I can't discuss it now, and anyway I'm not working for you, but I think this will require a conference of everyone concerned. Please tell Mr. Rollins that he will be expected at a meeting at my office at nine o'clock this evening. I'll invite the others, and I invite you now. At my office at nine o'clock, unless you hear otherwise."

"But what are we going—"

"No, Mr. Heery. You must excuse me. I'm busy. Goodbye, sir."

We hung up, and he turned to the company. "Mr. Rollins got one too and took it to Mr. Heery. It may reasonably be presumed that the other two—Miss Frazee and Miss Tescher—were not excluded. You heard what I said about a meeting here at nine o'clock this evening, and we shall want you with us. You'll come?"

"We're here now," Younger said. "This blows the whole thing sky high and you know it. Why put it off? Get them here now!"

"I don't want to wait until this evening," Mrs. Wheelock said, her voice so tense that I inspected her for signs of trembling, but saw none.

"You'll have to, madam." Wolfe was blunt. "I have to digest this strange finesse, and consult my clients." He looked up at the clock. "Only nine hours."

"You never answered my question," she complained. "Must I show this to the police and let them take it?" Her sheet was in her hand, and Younger had his.

"As you please—or rather, as you will. If you don't, when they learn that you got it, as of course they will, they'll be ruffled, but they are already. Suit yourself."

I was up and halfway to the door, to escort them out, but they weren't coming. They wanted to know what was what, then and there. Younger was so stubborn that I finally had to take his arm and put a little pressure on, and by the time I got him to the front, with his hat and coat on, and over the threshold to the stoop, he was in no humor to offer me a drink. They left together, and I hoped Younger would give Mrs. Wheelock a lift back to the hotel. She didn't have the physique or the vigor for a midtown bus.

I returned to the office and told Wolfe, "I know you like to do your own digesting, but one thing occurs to me. As far as the contest is concerned, it no longer matters who lifted the wallet. They've all got the answers now and there'll have to be a new deal, so what's left of our job?"

He grunted. "We still have it. You know what I was hired to do."

"Yes, sir. I ought to. But what if the client has lost interest in what you were hired to do?"

"We'll handle that contingency when we face it. For the immediate present there is enough to occupy us. I told you that with such tension something was sure to snap, though I must confess that I hadn't listed this among the possibilities. You will phone the others, all of them, and notify them of the meeting this evening, but from the kitchen or your room. I have to work. I haven't the slightest idea what course to take at the meeting, and I must contrive one. Now that this has happened we must move quickly, or you will be quite right—there will be no job left. I may need—confound it!"

The phone was ringing. I had it off the cradle automatically before remembering that my base of operations had been moved. An urgent male voice gave me not a request but an order, and I covered the transmitter and turned to Wolfe. "Buff. Exploding. You and only you."

He reached for his receiver. I stayed with mine.

15

"**N**ero Wolfe spea—"

"This is Buff. Is your wire tapped?"

"Not to my knowledge. I think we must assume it isn't, just as we assume an atom bomb won't interrupt us. Otherwise life becomes—"

"I couldn't reach Hansen so I got you." Buff's words were piling up. "A city detective is here, a Lieutenant Rowcliff, in my office. I came to another room to phone. He says that they have information that one of the contestants, Susan Tescher, received in the mail this morning a list of the answers to the five verses. Before he told me that he had asked me how many copies of the answers were in existence, and I told him what we have been telling them all along, just the one in the safe deposit box as far as we know. We haven't mentioned the copy Goodwin took. But with that woman getting a copy in the mail, the police—"

"One moment, Mr. Buff. Three of the other contestants also received copies in the mail, and I suppose—"

"Three others! Then what—who sent them?"

"I don't know. I didn't, and Mr. Goodwin didn't."

"Where's the copy he took?"

"In the inner compartment of my safe. That's where he put it, and it must still be there. Hold the wire a moment while he looks."

I put my receiver down, went to the safe, swung the outer door open, and got at the dial of the four-way combination of the inner door. It takes a little time. Opening the door, there on top of the stack of papers I saw the leaves from my notebook. I took them out, made sure all four were there, returned them, shut the door and the outer door, announced to Wolfe, "Intact," and went back to my chair and picked up the receiver.

Wolfe spoke. "Mr. Buff? Mr. Goodwin's copy has remained in my safe and is there now. Mrs. Wheelock and

Mr. Younger have been to see me, and Mr. Heery has phoned me that Mr. Rollins was in his office. Have you heard from Mr. Heery?"

"Yes. He phoned Assa. We were just going to call you when this detective came. What's this about a meeting?"

"There will be one at nine o'clock this evening, at my office, for all those concerned. Mr. Goodwin was going—"

"That can wait." Buff was sounding more like a top executive than he had before. "What about the police? We've lied to them. We've told them that we know of no copy except the one in the safe deposit box. I have just repeated it to this detective. He's waiting in my office. What about it?"

"Well." Wolfe was judicious. "You were not under oath. The police have been lied to informally many times by many people, including me. The right to lie in the service of your own interests is highly valued and frequently exercised. However, the police are investigating a murder, and now the number of extant copies of the answers will be of vital concern to them. Hitherto they would have been annoyed at discovery of your lie; if you fail to disclose it now and they discover it later they will be enraged. I suggest that you disclose it immediately."

"Admit we all lied?"

"Certainly. There is no depravity attached and there can be no penalty. No man should tell a lie unless he is shrewd enough to recognize the time for renouncing it, if and when it comes, and knows how to renounce it gracefully. About the meeting this evening—"

"We can discuss that later. I'll call you."

He was off. Wolfe cradled the receiver, pushed the phone to one side, heaved a sigh clear down to where a strip of his yellow shirt showed between his vest and pants, as usual, leaned back, and shut his eyes.

"Of course you know," I said, "that that will bring us company."

"It can't be helped," he muttered.

Since the phone numbers of LBA and the Churchill were in my head, the only ones I had to scribble in my notebook were *Clock* magazine and Hansen's and Heery's offices. That done, I went to the kitchen, where Fritz was putting some lamb hearts to soak in sour milk and an assortment of herbs and spices, asked if I could use his phone, and started in. Four of them—Wheelock, Younger, Heery, and Buff—had already been invited and would get a reminder call later. Presumably Rollins had also been invited, but that had to be checked. I got two of them without much difficulty, O'Garro and Assa, on one call, but had a hell of a time with the others. Four different calls to Gertrude Frazee's room, eighteen-fourteen, at the Churchill, in a period of forty minutes, got me no answer. Three calls failed to land Rudolph Hansen, but he finally called back, and of course had to speak to Wolfe. I stood pat that he couldn't, and though he refused to accept the invitation to the meeting, I knew nothing could keep him away. I also got Harold Rollins, who told me in one short superior sentence that he would be present and hung up.

Susan Tescher was a tough one. First *Clock* told me she was in conference. Then *Clock* said she wasn't there today. I asked for Mr. Knudsen, the tall and bony one, but he had stepped out. I asked for Mr. Schultz, the tall and broad one, and he was engaged. I asked for Mr. Hibbard, the tall and skinny one, of the legal staff, and darned if I didn't get him. I told him about the meeting, and who would be there, and said that if Miss Tescher didn't come she might find herself tomorrow morning confronted with a *fait accompli,* knowing as I did that any lawyer would feel that a guy who used words like *fait accompli* was a man to be reckoned with. As I was starting to dial the Churchill number for another stab at Miss Frazee, the doorbell rang. I went to the hall for a look through the panel, then opened the door to the office. Apparently Wolfe hadn't moved a muscle.

I announced, "Stebbins."

He opened his eyes. "At least it's better than Mr. Cramer. Bring him in."

I went and unbolted the door, swung it wide, and said hospitably, "Hello there. We've been waiting for you."

"I'll bet you have." He marched on by me, making quite an air wash, and on by the rack, removing his hat as he entered the office. By the time I attended to the door and caught up he was standing in front of Wolfe's desk and talking. ". . . the copy of the contest answers that Goodwin made last Wednesday. Where is it?"

If you want to see Purley Stebbins at his worst you should see him with Nero Wolfe. He knows that on the record of the evidence, of which there is plenty, Wolfe is more than a match for him and Cramer put together, and by his training and experience evidence is all that counts, but he can't believe it and he won't. The result is that he talks too loud and too fast. I have seen Purley at work with different kinds of characters, taking his time with both his head and his tongue, and he's not bad at all. He hates to come at Wolfe, so he always comes himself instead of passing the buck.

Wolfe muttered at him, "Sit down, Mr. Stebbins. As you know, I don't like to stretch my neck."

That was the sort of thing. Purley would have liked to say, "To hell with your neck," and nearly did, but blocked it and lowered himself onto a chair. He never took the red leather one.

Wolfe looked at me. "Archie, tell him about the copy you made."

I obliged. "Last Wednesday I went to the safe deposit vault with Buff, O'Garro, and Heery. They got the box and opened it. I cut the two envelopes open, one with the verses and one with the answers, and made copies on four sheets from my notebook. The originals were returned to the envelopes, and the envelopes to the box, and the box to the vault. I came straight home with my copies and put them in the safe as soon as I got here, and they've been there ever since and are there now."

"I want to see them," Purley rasped.

Wolfe answered him. "No, sir. It would serve no purpose unless you handled and inspected them, and if you got hold of them you wouldn't let go. It would be meaningless anyway. Since Mr. Buff decided to tell about them we knew you would be coming, and if anything had happened to them Mr. Goodwin could have made duplicates and put them in the safe. No. We tell you they are there."

"They've been there all the time since Goodwin put them there last Wednesday?"

"Yes. Continuously."

"You haven't had them out once?"

"No."

Purley turned his big weathered face to me. "Have you?"

"Nope.—Wait a minute, I have too. An hour ago. Buff was on the phone and asked where they were, and Mr.

Wolfe told me to take a look to make sure. I took them out and glanced over them, and put them right back. That was the only time I've had them out of the safe since I put them in."

His head jerked back to Wolfe and he barked, "Then what the hell did you get 'em for?"

Wolfe nodded. "That's a good question. To answer it adequately I would have to go back to that day and recall all of my impressions and surmises and tentative designs, and I'm busy and haven't time. So I'll only say that I had certain vague notions which never ripened. That will have to do you."

Purley's jaw was working. "What I think," he said.

"I beg your pardon?"

"I said, what I think. So does the Inspector. He wanted to come, but he was late for an appointment with the Commissioner, so he sent me. We think you sent the copies of the answers to the contestants." He clamped the jaw. He released it. "Or we think you might have, and we want to know. I don't have to tell you what it means to this murder investigation, whether you did it or not—hell, I don't have to tell you anything. I ask you a straight question: did you send copies of those answers to the contestants?"

"No, sir."

"Do you know who did?"

"No, sir."

Purley came to me. "Did you send them?"

"No."

"Do you know who did?"

"No."

"I think you're both lying," he growled. That was an instance. He was talking too fast.

Wolfe lifted his shoulders and dropped them. "After that," he said, "conversation becomes pointless."

"Yeah, I know it does." Purley swallowed. "I take it back. I take it back because I want to ask a favor. The Inspector told me not to. He said if Goodwin typed those copies he wouldn't have used his machine here, and he may be right, but I hereby request you to let me type something on that typewriter"—he aimed a thumb—"and take it with me. Well?"

"Certainly," Wolfe agreed. "It's rather impudent, but

102

I prefer that to prolonging the conversation. I'm busy and it's nearly lunch time. Archie?"

I pulled the machine to me, rolled some paper in, and vacated the chair, and Purley came and took it and started banging. He used forefingers only but made fair time. I stood back of his shoulder and watched him run it off:

```
Many minimum men came running and the
quick brown fox jumped over the lazy moon
and now is the time for all good men to
come to the aid of the party 234567890-
ASDFGHJKL:QWERTY UIOPZXCVBNM?
```

When he had rolled it out and was folding it I said helpfully, "By the way, I've got an old machine up in my room that I use sometimes. You should have a sample of that too. Come on."

That was a mistake, because if I hadn't said it I probably would have had the pleasure of hearing him thank Wolfe for something, which would have been a first. Instead, "Hang 'em on your nose and snap at 'em," he told me, retrieved his hat from the floor beside his chair, and tramped out. By the time I got to the hall he had the front door open. He didn't pull it shut after him, which I thought was rather petty for a sergeant. I went and closed and bolted it, and returned to the office.

Wolfe was at the bookshelves, returning Casanova and Dorothy Osborne and the others to their places. Since it was only ten minutes to lunch time, he couldn't have been expected to get back to work. I stood and watched him.

"Apparently," I said, "the rules have been changed, but you might have told me. It has never been put into words, but I have always understood that when you want to keep something to yourself you may choke me off with a smoke screen but you don't tell me a direct lie. You may lie to others in my presence, and often have, but not to me when we're alone. So I believed you when you said the contestants getting the answers in the mail was a surprise to you. I'm not griping, I'm just saying I think it would be a good idea to let me know when you change the rules."

He finished slipping the last book in, nice and even

103

with the edge of the shelf, and turned. "I haven't changed the rules."

"Then have I been wrong all along? Is it okay for you to tell me a direct lie when we're alone?"

"No. It never has been."

"And it isn't now?"

"No."

"You haven't lied to me about the answers?"

"No."

"I see. Then I'd better keep everybody off your neck this afternoon. If you haven't already got a program for tonight's meeting, and evidently you haven't, I'm glad it's up to you and not me."

I went to my desk and rolled the typewriter back in place, to have something to do. I like to think I can see straight, and during the past hour or so I had completely sold myself on the idea that I knew now what Saul Panzer's errand had been; and I don't like to buy a phony, especially from myself. Pushing the typewriter stand back, I banged it against the edge of my desk, not intentionally, and Wolfe looked at me in surprise.

16

By four o'clock everybody was set for the evening party with one exception. Wheelock, Younger, Buff, and Heery had been reminded. O'Garro, Assa, Rollins, and Hansen didn't need to be. As for Susan Tescher, Hibbard had called and said she would be present provided he could come along, and I said we'd be glad to have him. The exception was Gertrude Frazee. I tried her five times after lunch, three times from the kitchen and twice from my room, and didn't get her.

When, at four o'clock, Fritz and I heard Wolfe's elevator ascending to the roof, we went to the office and made some preliminary preparations. There would be ten of them, eleven if I got Frazee, so chairs had to be brought from the front room and dining room. Wolfe had said there should be refreshments, so a table had to be placed at the end of the couch, covered with a yellow linen cloth, with napkins and other accessories. Fritz had already started on canapés and other snacks and filling the vacuum bucket with ice cubes. There was no need to check the supply of liquids, since Wolfe does that himself at least once a week. He hates to have anybody, even a policeman or a woman, ask for something he hasn't got. When we had things under control Fritz returned to the kitchen and I went to my desk and got at the phone for another try for Frazee.

By gum, I got her, no trouble at all. Her own voice, and she admitted she remembered me. She was a little frosty, asking me what I wanted, but I overlooked it.

"I'm calling," I said, "to ask you to join us at a gathering at Mr. Wolfe's office at nine o'clock this evening. The other contestants will be here, and Mr. Heery, and members of the firm of Lippert, Buff and Assa."

"What's it for?"

"To discuss the situation as it stands now. Since the contestants have received a list of the answers from some unknown source, there must be—"

"I haven't received any answers from any source, known or unknown. I'm expecting word Wednesday morning from my friends at home, and I'll have my answers in by the deadline. I've heard enough of this trick."

She was gone.

I cradled the phone, sat and gave it a thought, buzzed the plant rooms on the house phone, and got Wolfe.

"Do you want Miss Frazee here tonight?" I asked him.

"I want all of them here. I said so."

"Yeah, I heard you. Then I'll have to go get her. She just told me on the phone that she hasn't received any answers and she's heard enough of this trick. And hung up. If she's clean, she tore up the envelope and paper and flushed them down the toilet, and she's standing pat. Do you want her?"

"Yes. Phone again?"

"No good. She's not in a mood to chat."

"Then you'll have to go."

I said okay, went to the kitchen to ask Fritz to come and bolt after me, got my hat and coat, and left.

The clock above the bank of elevators at the Churchill

said five-seventeen. On the way up in the taxi I had considered three different approaches and hadn't cared much for any of them, so my mind was occupied and I didn't notice the guy who entered the elevator just before the door closed and backed up against me. But when he got out at the eighteenth, as I did, and crossed over to the floor clerk and told her, "Miss Frazee, eighteen-fourteen," I took a look and recognized him. It was Bill Lurick of the *Gazette,* who is assigned to milder matters than homicide only when there are no homicides on tap. I thought, By God, she's been croaked, and stepped on it to catch up with him, on his way down the hall, and told him hello.

He stopped. "Hi, Goodwin. You in on this? What's up?"

"Search me. I'm taking magazine subscriptions. What brought you?"

"Always cagey. The subtle elusive type. Not me, ask me a question I answer it." He moved on. "We got word that Miss Gertrude Frazee would hold a press conference."

Of course that was a gag, but when we turned the corner and came to eighteen-fourteen, and I got a look inside through the open door, it wasn't. There were three males and one female in sight, and I knew two of them: Al Riordan of the Associated Press and Missy Coburn of the *World-Telegram.* Lurick asked a man standing just inside if he had missed anything, and the man said no, she insisted on waiting until the *Times* got there, and Lurick said that was proper, they wouldn't start Judgment Day until the *Times* was set to cover. A man approached down the hall and exchanged greetings, and entered, and somebody said, "All right, Miss Frazee. This is Charles Winston of the *Times.*"

Her voice came: "The *New York Times?*"

"Correct. All others are imitations. Do you think one of the contestants killed Louis Dahlmann?"

"I don't know and I don't care." I couldn't see her, but she kept her voice up and spoke distinctly. "I asked you to come here because the American public ought to know, especially American women, that a gigantic swindle is being perpetrated. I have been accused by three people of getting a list of the contest answers in the mail, and it's not true. They say the other contestants got lists of the

106

answers too, and I don't know whether they did or not, but they have no right to accuse me. It's an insult to American women. It's a trick to wreck the contest and get out of paying the prizes to those who have earned them, and it's a despicable thing to do. And it's me they want to cheat. They're afraid of all the publicity the Women's Nature League is getting at last, they're afraid American women will begin to listen to our great message—"

"Excuse me, Miss Frazee. We need the facts. Who are the three people that accused you?"

"One was a policeman, not in uniform, I don't know his name. One was a man named Hansen, a lawyer, I think his first name is Rudolph, he represents the contest people. The third was a man named Goodwin, Archie Goodwin, he works for that detective, Nero Wolfe. They're all in it together. It's a dirty conspiracy to—"

I had my notebook out, along with the journalists, chiefly for the novelty of participating in a press conference without paying dues to the American Newspaper Guild, and I got it all down, but I doubt if it's worth passing on. It developed into a seesaw. She wanted to concentrate on the Women's Nature League, of which they had already had several doses, and they wanted to know about the alleged list of answers received by the contestants, which would have rated the front page on account of its bearing on the murder if they could nail it down. But they couldn't very well get the nail from her, since she was claiming she had never got such a list and knew nothing about it. They kept working on her anyway until Lurick suddenly exclaimed, "Hey, Goodwin's right here!" and headed for the door.

Instead of retreating, I crossed the sill and got my back against the open door, since the main point was to make sure that it didn't get closed with me on the wrong side. They all came at me and hemmed me in so that I didn't have elbow room to put my notebook in my pocket, all demanding to know if the contestants had received a list of the answers, and if so, when and how and from whom?

I regarded them as friends. It is always best to regard journalists as friends if they are not actually standing on your nose. "Hold everything," I said. "What kind of a position is a man in when he is being tugged in two directions?"

Charles Winston of the *Times* said, "Anomalous."

"Thanks. That's the word I wanted. I would love to get my name in the paper, and my employer's name, Nero Wolfe, spelled with an e on the end, and this is a swell chance, but I'll have to pass it up. As you all saw at once, if the contestants have been sent a list of the answers by somebody it would be a hot item in a murder case, and it would be improper for me to tell you about it. That's the function of the police and the District Attorney."

"Oh, come off it, Archie," Missy Coburn said.

"Spit out the gum," Bill Lurick said.

"Is it your contention," Charles Winston of the *Times* asked courteously but firmly, "that a private citizen should refuse to furnish the press with any information regarding a murder case and that the sole source of such information for the public should be the duly constituted authorities?"

I didn't want to get the *Times* sore. "Listen, folks," I said, "there is a story to be had, but you're not going to get it from me, for reasons which I reserve for the present, so don't waste time and breath on me. Try Inspector Cramer or the DA's office. You heard Miss Frazee mention Rudolph Hansen, the lawyer. I've told you there's a story, so that's settled, but you'll have to take it from there. Cigarettes on my bare toes will get you no more from me."

They hung on some, but pretty soon one of them broke away and headed down the hall, and of course the others didn't want him to gobble it so they made after him. I stayed in the doorway until the last of them had disappeared around the corner, then, leaving the door open, turned and went on in. Gertrude Frazee, in the same museum outfit she had worn five days previously, minus the hat, was in an upholstered armchair backed up against the wall, with a cold eye on me.

She spoke. "I have nothing to say to you. You can go. Please shut the door."

I had forgotten that her lips moving at right angles to their slant, and her jaw moving straight up and down, made an anomalous situation, and I had to jerk my attention to her words. "You must admit one thing, Miss Frazee," I said earnestly. "I didn't try to spoil your press conference, did I? I kept out of it, and when they came at me what did I do? I refused to tell them a single thing, because I thought it wouldn't be fair to you. It was your conference and I had no right to horn in."

She didn't thaw any. "What do you want?"

"Nothing now, I guess. I was going to explain why I thought you might want to come to the meeting this evening at Mr. Wolfe's office, but now I suppose you wouldn't be interested."

"Why not?"

"Because you've already got your lick in. Not only that, you've spilled the beans. Outsiders weren't supposed to know about the meeting, especially not the press, but now those reporters will be after everybody, and they're sure to find out, and they'll be camping on Mr. Wolfe's stoop. I wouldn't be surprised if they even got invited in. The others will know they've heard your side of the story, and naturally they'll want to get theirs in too. So if you were there it might get into a wrangle in front of the reporters, and you wouldn't want that. Anyhow, as I say, you've already got your lick in."

With her unique facial design nothing could be certain, but I was pretty sure I had her, so I finished, "So I guess you wouldn't be interested and I've made the trip for nothing. Sorry to bother you. If you care at all to know what happens at the meeting, see the morning papers, especially the *Times*." I was turning to go.

Her voice halted me. "Young man."

I faced her.

"What time is this meeting?"

"Nine o'clock."

"I'll be there."

"Sure, Miss Frazee, if you want to, but under the circumstances I doubt—"

"I'll be there."

I grinned at her. "I promised my grandmother I'd never argue with a lady. See you later then."

Leaving, I took the door along, pulling it shut gently until the lock clicked.

By the time I got home it was after six and Wolfe

should have been down from the plant rooms, but he wasn't. I went to the kitchen, where Fritz was arranging two plump ducklings on the rack of a roasting pan, asked what was up, and was told that Wolfe had descended from the roof but had left the elevator one flight up and gone to his room. That was unusual but not alarming, and I proceeded with another step of the preparations for the meeting. When I got through the table at the end of the couch in the office was ready for business: eight brands of whisky, two of gin, two of cognac, a decanter of port, cream sherry, armagnac, four fruit brandies, and a wide assortment of cordials and liqueurs. The dry sherry was in the refrigerator, as were the cherries, olives, onions, and lemon peel, where they would remain until after dinner. As I was arranging the bottles I caught myself wondering which one the murderer would fancy, but corrected it hastily to wallet thief, since we weren't interested in the murder.

At six-thirty I thought I'd better find out if Wolfe had busted a shoestring or what, and, mounting a flight and tapping on his door and hearing him grunt, entered. I stopped and stared. Fully dressed, with his shoes on, he was lying on the bed, on top of the black silk coverlet. Absolutely unheard of.

"What have you got?" I demanded.

"Nothing," he growled.

"Shall I get Doc Vollmer?"

"No."

I approached for a close-up. He looked sour, but he had never died of that. "Miss Frazee is coming," I told him. "She was holding a press conference. Do you want to hear about it?"

"No."

"Excuse me for disturbing you," I said icily, and turned to go, but in three steps he called my name and I halted. He raised himself to his elbows, swung his legs over the edge, got upright, and took a deep breath.

"I've made a bad mistake," he said.

I waited.

He took another breath. "What time is it?"

I told him twenty-five to seven.

"Two hours and a half and dinner to eat. I was confident that this development would of itself supply me with ample material for an effective stratagem, and I was wrong. I don't say I was an ass. I relied overmuch on my ingenuity and resourcefulness, though on the solid basis of experience. But I did make a mistake. Various people have been trying to see me all afternoon, and I have declined to see them. I thought I could devise a stroke without any hint or stimulant from them, but I haven't. I should have seen them. Oh, I can proceed; I am not without expedients; I may even bring something off; but I blundered. Just now you asked me if I wanted to hear about Miss Frazee, and I said no. That was fatuous. Tell me."

"Yes, sir. As I said, she was holding a press conference. When I got there——"

The sound of the doorbell came up and in to us. I lifted my brows at Wolfe. He snapped at me, "Go! Anybody!"

17

It was Vernon Assa. He wasn't as much of a misfit for the red leather chair as Mrs. Wheelock, at least he was plump, and his deep tan went well with the red, but he was much too short. I have surveyed a lot of people in that chair, and there has only been one who was exactly right for it. I must tell about him some time.

You might have thought, after what had just been said upstairs, that Wolfe would have been spreading butter on the caller, but he wasn't. When he came down, after brushing his hair and tucking his shirt in, he crossed to his chair, sat, and said brusquely, "I can spare a few minutes, Mr. Assa. What can I do for you?"

Assa looked at me. I thought he was going to start the old routine about seeing Wolfe privately, but apparently he only wanted something attractive to look at while he got his words collected. I remembered that at the first visit of the LBA bunch he had been the impatient one, snapping at Hansen to get on and telling Wolfe he was wasting time, but now he seemed to feel that deliberation was better.

He looked at Wolfe. "About the meeting this evening. You'll have to call it off."

"Indeed." Wolfe cocked his head. "Under what compulsion?"

"Well . . . it's obvious. Isn't it?"

"Not to me. I'm afraid you'll have to elaborate."

Assa shifted in the chair. I had noticed that he seemed to be having trouble getting comfortably adjusted. "You realize," he said, "that our main problem is solved, thanks to you. The problem that brought us to you last Wednesday in a state of panic. There was no chance of finishing the contest without confusion and some discord after what happened to Dahlmann, and the wallet gone, but as it looked when we came to you we were headed for complete disaster, and you have prevented it. Hansen is certain that legally we are in the clear. With the contestants receiving the answers as they have, and it won't do Miss Frazee any good to deny she got them, if we repudiate those verses and replace them with others, as of course we will, our position would be upheld by any court in the land. There is still serious embarrassment, but that couldn't be helped. You have rescued the contest from utter ruin by a brilliant stroke and are to be congratulated."

"Mr. Assa." Wolfe's eyes, on him, were half closed. "Are you speaking for my client, the firm of Lippert, Buff and Assa, or for yourself?"

"Well . . . I am a member of the firm, as you know, but I came here on my own initiative and responsibility."

"Do your associates know you're here and what for?"

"No. I didn't want to start a long and complicated discussion. I decided to come only half an hour ago. Your meeting starts at nine, and it's nearly seven now."

"I see. And you are assuming that I sent the answers to the contestants—or had them sent."

Assa passed his tongue over his lips. "I didn't put it baldly like that, but I suppose it doesn't matter. Goodwin is in your confidence anyway. It was impossible to figure why one of the contestants would have sent them, if he had killed Dahlmann and got them from the wallet, and that leaves only you."

"Not impossible," Wolfe objected. "Not if he found to his dismay that in the situation he had created they were worse than useless to him."

Assa nodded. "I considered that, of course, but still thought it impossible. Another reason I didn't mention my coming to my associates was that I realize you can't acknowledge what you did to save us. I don't expect you to acknowledge it even to me, and you certainly wouldn't if one or two of them had come along, especially Hansen. We wouldn't want you to acknowledge it anyhow, because we've hired you, and the legal position would probably be that we did it ourselves, and that would be disastrous. So you see why I didn't put it baldly."

"Thank you for your forbearance," Wolfe said drily. "But why must the meeting be called off?"

"Because it can't do any good and may do harm. What good can it do?"

Wolfe's eyes were still half closed. "It can help me to earn a fee. I accepted Mr. Hansen's definition of my job: 'to find out who took the wallet and got the paper.' It remains to be performed."

"It doesn't have to be performed, not now, since the contest problem is solved. You've earned your fee and you'll get it."

"You've admitted, Mr. Assa, that you're speaking only for yourself."

The red tip of his tongue showed again, flicking his lips. "I'll guarantee the fee," he said.

Wolfe shook his head. "I'm afraid that's not acceptable. My responsibility is to my client, and his reciprocal responsibility, to pay me, is not transferable. As for canceling the meeting, that's out of the question. If such a request came unanimously from Messrs. Buff, O'Garro, Hansen, Heery—and you, and cogent reasons were given, I might consider it, but would probably refuse. As it is, I won't even consider it."

Assa looked at me. He glanced at the refreshment table, came back to me, and said, "There's a bottle of Pernod there. That's my drink. Could I have some?"

I said certainly and asked if he wanted ice, and he said no. I took him the Pernod and an Old-Fashioned glass, and he poured two fingers as plump as his own, and darned if he didn't toss it off as if it were a jigger of bourbon. I'm not a Pernod drinker, but there is such a thing as common sense. Not only that, he poured again, this time only one finger, and then, without taking a sip, put the glass down on the little table at his elbow, beside the bottle.

He swallowed a couple of times for a chaser. "That's a highhanded attitude, Mr. Wolfe," he said. He paused to collect more words. "Frankly, I don't see what you expect to accomplish. You'll get your fee, and from our standpoint, as far as the contest is concerned, it no longer matters who got the wallet. Of course it may still be a factor in the murder, but you weren't hired to investigate the murder. That's up to the police. Why do you insist on this meeting?"

"To finish my job. What I engaged to do."

"But you're more apt to undo what you've already done. The police know now—they were told on your advice—that you have had a copy of the answers in your possession since last Wednesday. How far the discretion of the police can be trusted I don't know, but it's conceivable that one or more of the contestants have learned about it, and if so, God only knows what would happen at the meeting. You might even find yourself backed into a corner where you had to admit you had mailed the answers to them, and LBA would be responsible, and we'd be in a deeper hole than ever."

"You would indeed," Wolfe conceded. "But if that's your fear, dismiss it. There will be no such admission by me."

"What will there be?"

"I couldn't tell you if I would. I have formed certain conjectures and I intend to explore them. That's what the meeting is for, and I shall not abandon it."

Assa regarded him in silence, steadily, for a full half a minute. At length he broke it. "When your man Goodwin came to our office on Friday and got the word for you to go ahead, he wanted it unanimous. He polled us, and I voted yes with the others. Now I don't, so it's no longer unanimous. I ask you to suspend operations until I have conferred with my associates—say until tomorrow noon. I not only ask you, I direct you."

Wolfe was shaking his head. "I'm afraid I can't oblige

you, Mr. Assa. Time's important now, now that the spark has been struck and the fire started. It's too late."

"Too late for what?"

"To stop."

Assa's eyes dropped. He gazed at his right palm, saw nothing there to encourage him, tried the left, and there was nothing there either. "Very well," he said, and arose, in no haste, and started for the door. Considering the turn things had taken, I wouldn't have been astonished if Wolfe had told me to fasten onto him and lock him in the front room until nine o'clock, but he didn't, so I got up and followed the guest into the hall. I didn't resent his not thanking me for holding his topcoat and opening the door, since he was obviously preoccupied.

Back in the office, I stood and looked down at Wolfe. "I suppose," I observed, "it doesn't matter who struck the spark as long as it caught."

"Yes. Get Mr. Cramer."

I sat at my desk and dialed. It was a bad time of day to get Cramer ordinarily, but when something big was stirring, or refusing to stir, he sometimes ate at his desk instead of going home for what he called supper. That was one of the times. From the way he growled at me, it was very much one of the times.

Wolfe took it. "Mr. Cramer? I thought you might be interested in a meeting at my office this evening. We're going to discuss the Dahlmann case. It will—"

"Who's going to discuss it?"

"Everyone concerned—that is, everyone I know about. It will of course be confined to the theft of the wallet, since that's what I'm investigating, but it will inevitably touch upon points that affect you, so I'm inviting you to come—as an observer."

Silence. Cramer could have been chewing a bite of a corned beef sandwich, or he could have been chewing what he had heard.

"What have you got?" he demanded.

"For myself, a reasonable expectation. For you, the possibility of a suitable disclosure. Have I ever wasted your time on frivolity?"

"No. Not on frivolity. There's no use asking you on the phone. . . . Stebbins will be there in ten minutes."

115

"No, sir. Nor you. I need a little time to arrange the inside of my head, and my dinner will be ready shortly. The meeting will be at nine o'clock."

"I'll bring Stebbins with me."

"By all means. Do so."

We hung up.

"You know darned well," I said, "that Purley will bring handcuffs, and he hates to take them back empty——"

I stopped because he was leaning back and closing his eyes, and his lips were starting to move, pushing out and then in, out and in. . . . He was working at last. I went across the hall for two more chairs.

18

If a successful party is one where everybody comes, there was no question about that one. In fact, some came too early. Gertrude Frazee showed up at eight-thirty-five, when Wolfe and I were still in the dining room, and I was having coffee in the office with her when Philip Younger arrived, and a minute later Talbott Heery. Patrick O'Garro and Oliver Buff came together, and almost on their heels Professor Harold Rollins. When Inspector Cramer and Sergeant Stebbins got there it was still ten minutes short of nine. They wanted to see Wolfe immediately, of course, and I took them to the dining room and shut them in there with him. Back at the front door, I opened it for Vernon Assa, who was still in no frame of mind to thank anybody for anything, and then for Susan Tescher, of *Clock* magazine. I had been sort of hoping to see Mr. Tite himself, but all she had along was Mr. Hibbard, the tall and skinny one. It was nine on the dot when Mrs. Wheelock appeared, and not more than thirty seconds later here came Rudolph Hansen. Not only did everybody come, they all beat the bell except Hansen, and he just shaved it.

I went to glance in at the office door and saw that Fritz had things under control at the refreshment table. Evidently they had all been thirsty, or else they didn't want to talk and were drinking instead. Pleased that the party was starting well, I crossed to the dining room to tell Wolfe we had a full house and were set for his entrance, but, entering, I shut the door and stood. Cramer, sitting with his big rough fist tapping the table, was reading Wolfe the riot act, with Purley standing behind his shoulder looking satisfied. I approached. What seemed to be biting Cramer was that he did not intend to let Wolfe call a meeting of murder suspects and expect him, Cramer, to sit and take it in like a goddam stenographer (Cramer's words, not mine; I have known at least three stenographers who were absolutely—anyway, I have known stenographers).

I had heard Cramer lose that argument with Wolfe some twenty times. What he wanted was the moon. He wanted, first, to know in advance exactly what Wolfe was going to say, which was ridiculous because most of the time Wolfe didn't know himself. Second, he wanted it understood that he would be free to take over at any point, bound by no commitment, whereas Wolfe demanded a pledge that the proceedings would be left to him short of extreme provocation, such as gunplay or hair pulling. Since it was a cinch that Cramer wouldn't have been there at all if he hadn't thought Wolfe had something he badly needed, he might as well have given up on that one for good, but he never did. All he accomplished that Monday evening was holding up the start of the meeting by a quarter of an hour. I cut in on the squabble to announce that the audience was ready and waiting, and then went to the office.

A few details needed attention. Miss Frazee had copped the red leather chair, which was reserved for Inspector Cramer, and I had to talk her into moving. Buff and Hansen were in a huddle at the wall end of the couch, where Wolfe would have to look through me to see them, and I got them to transfer to chairs, Buff stopping on the way for a refill of his highball glass. Hibbard was seated beside Miss Tescher in the front row, and when I asked him to move to the rear I thought he was going to speak at last, but he controlled it and went without a word. Vernon Assa bothered me. He was standing backed up against the far wall, staring straight ahead, an Old-

Fashioned glass in his hand, presumably holding Pernod. When I went to him he turned his eyes on me and I didn't like them. He could have been high, too high, but when I suggested that he come and take a chair he said in a perfectly good voice that he was all right where he was. As I turned to leave him Wolfe and Cramer and Stebbins entered.

Wolfe walked across to his desk. Cramer stood a moment taking in the crowd and then went to the red leather chair and sat. I had put a chair for Purley against the wall, so he would be facing the audience, and he didn't need to be told it was his. The talking had stopped, and all eyes went to Wolfe as he rested his clasped hands on the desk and moved his head from left to right and back again.

He took a breath. "Ladies and gentlemen. I must first . explain the presence of Inspector Cramer of the New York Police Department. He is here by invitation, not to—"

Two sounds came almost simultaneously from the rear of the room—first from a throat, part gurgle and part scream, and then a bang as something hit the floor. Everybody jerked around by reflex, so we all saw Vernon Assa stagger toward us with the fingers of both hands clutching at his mouth, and then he went down. By the time he touched the floor I was there, but Purley Stebbins was right behind me, and Cramer behind him, so I dived back to my desk for the phone and dialed Doc Vollmer's number. At the second buzz he answered and I told him to come on the jump. As I hung up Cramer called to me to get a doctor and I told him I had one. He stood up, saw Susan Tescher and Hibbard crossing the sill into the hall, and sang out, "Get back in here!" He came to me. "I'll call downtown. Put 'em all in the dining room and stay there with 'em. Understand? No gags." He was at the phone.

I looked around. They were behaving pretty well, except Susan Tescher and her silent partner, who had apparently had the notion of fading. There had been no shrieks. Wolfe was sitting straight, his lips pressed tight, his eyes narrowed to slits. He didn't meet my glance. O'Garro and Heery and Hansen had gone to the prostrate Assa, but

118

Purley, kneeling there, had ordered them back. I went to the doorway to the hall and turned.

"Everybody this way," I said. No one moved. "I'd rather not yell," I said, "because the inspector's phoning. He wants you out of this room, and four of the men will please bring chairs."

That helped, giving them something to do. Philip Younger picked up a chair and came, and the others after him. I opened the door to the dining room, and they filed across and in. Fritz was at my elbow, and I told him there would be lots of company and he might as well leave the bolt off. The doorbell rang, and he went and admitted Doc Vollmer, and I waved Doc to the office.

Leaving the door from the dining room to the hall wide open and standing just inside, I surveyed my herd. Mrs. Wheelock had flopped onto a chair, and so had Philip Younger. I hoped Younger wasn't having a paroxysm. Most of the others were standing, and I told them they might as well sit down.

The only one who put up a squawk was Rudolph Hansen. He confronted me. "Vernon Assa is my client and my friend, and I have a right to see that he gets proper—"

"He's already got. A doctor's here, and a good one." I raised my voice. "Just take it easy, everybody, and it would be better if you'd shut up."

"What happened to him?" Gertrude Frazee demanded.

"I don't know. But if you want something to occupy your minds, just before Mr. Wolfe entered he was standing by the wall with a glass in his hand and there was liquid in the glass. You heard the glass hit the floor, but I saw no sign of spilled liquid. You might turn that over and see what you think of it."

"It was Pernod in the glass," Patrick O'Garro said. "I saw him pour it. He always drank Pernod. He put the glass down on the table when Hansen called to him, and went—"

"Hold it, Pat," Hansen snapped at him. "This may be —I hope not—but this may be a very grave matter."

"You see," I told the herd. "I advised you to shut up, and Mr. Hansen, who is a lawyer, agrees with me."

"I want to telephone," Heery said.

"The phone's busy. Anyway, I'm just a temporary watchdog. I'll be getting a relief, and you can—"

I broke it off to stretch my neck for a look at the new-comers Fritz was admitting—two city employees in uniform. They came down the hall and headed for me, but I pointed across to the office and they right-angled. From there on it was a parade. A minute later two more in uniform came, and then three in their own clothes, two of whom I knew, and before long one with a little black bag. My herd had more or less settled down, and I had decided I didn't need to catch Doc Vollmer on his way out for a look at Younger. Two more arrived, and when I saw one of them was Lieutenant Rowcliff a little flutter ran over my biceps. He affects me that way. He and his pal went to the office, but pretty soon appeared again, heading for the dining room, and I sidestepped to keep from being trampled.

They entered, and the pal closed the door, and Rowcliff faced the herd. "You will remain here under surveillance until otherwise notified. Vernon Assa is dead. I am Lieutenant George Rowcliff, and for the present you are in my custody as material witnesses."

That was like him. In fact, it was him. What the hell did they care whether he was George Rowcliff or Cuthbert Rowcliff? Also he had said it wrong. If they were in his custody they were under arrest, and in that case they could demand to be allowed to communicate with their lawyers before answering any questions as a matter of ordinary prudence, which would stop the wheels of justice for hours. I was surprised that neither Hansen nor Hibbard picked it up, but they could have thought it would sound like soliciting business and didn't want to be unethical. Lawyers are very delicate.

I was in an anomalous position again. I wanted to open the door to leave, (a) to see if Wolfe wanted me, (b) to watch the scientists at work, and (c) to get a rise out of Rowcliff in case he had the notion that I was in his custody too, but on the other hand it seemed likely that a specimen who had had the nerve to commit a murder in Wolfe's office, right under his nose, was there in the dining room, and I didn't like to leave him with only a baboon like Rowcliff to keep an eye on him. I was propped against the wall, considering it, when the door opened and Inspector Cramer walked in. Short of the table he stopped and sent his eyes around.

120

"Mr. Buff," he said. "Buff and O'Garro and Hansen—and I guess Heery. You four men come here please." They moved. "Stand there in front of me. I'm going to show you something and ask if you can identify it. Look at it as close as you want to, but don't touch it. You understand? Don't touch it."

They said they understood, and he lifted a hand. The thumb and forefinger were pinching the corner of a brown leather wallet. The quartet gazed at it. O'Garro's hand started toward it and he jerked it back. No one spoke.

"The initials 'LD' are stamped on the inside," Cramer said, "and it contained items with Louis Dahlmann's name on them, but I'm asking if you can identify it as the wallet Dahlmann was carrying at that meeting last Tuesday evening."

"Of course not," Hansen said curtly. "Positively identify it? Certainly not."

A voice came from behind him: "It looks like it." Gertrude Frazee had stepped up to help. Rowcliff got her elbow to ease her back, but she made it stronger. "It looks exactly like it!"

"Okay," Cramer said, "I'm not asking you to swear to it, but you can tell me this, is it enough like the wallet he had at that meeting that you can't see any difference? I ask you that, Mr. Hansen."

"I can't answer. I wasn't at the meeting. Neither was Mr. Buff."

"Oh." Cramer wasn't fazed. Even an inspector can't remember everything. "You, Mr. O'Garro? You heard the question."

"Yes," O'Garro said.

"Mr. Heery?"

"It looks like it. Assa had it?"

Cramer nodded. "In his breast pocket."

"I knew it!" Miss Frazee cried. "A trick! A cheat! I knew all the time—"

Rowcliff gripped her arm, and she whirled and used the other one to smack him in the face, and I made a note to send a contribution to the Women's Nature League. Others started to ask Cramer things, or tell him, but he showed them a palm. "You'll all get a chance to talk before you leave here. Plenty. Stay here until you're sent for."

"Are we under arrest?" Harold Rollins asked, as superior as ever.

"No. You're being detained by police authority at the scene of a violent death in your presence. Anyone who prefers to be arrested will be accommodated." He turned, looked around for me, found me, said, "Come with me, Goodwin," and made for the door.

19

I supposed he was taking me to the office, but no, he told me to wait in the hall, and anyway there wasn't room for me in the office. A mob of experts was expertizing in every direction, and Fritz was seated in Wolfe's chair behind his desk, watching them. Wolfe was nowhere in sight. From the door I saw Cramer go to one sitting at my desk and deliver the wallet by depositing it gently in a little box. Then he passed a few orders around, came to me and said, "Wolfe's up in his room," and headed up the stairs. I followed.

Wolfe's door was closed, but Cramer opened it without bothering to knock, and walked in. That was bad manners. He was unquestionably in command of the office, since a man had just died there violently with him present, but not the rest of the house. However, it wasn't the best possible moment to read him the Bill of Rights, so I followed him in and shut the door.

At least Wolfe hadn't gone to bed. He was in the big chair under the reading lamp with a book. Lifting his eyes to us, he put the book on the table, and as I moved a chair up for Cramer I caught its title: *Montaigne's Essays*. It was one of a few dozen he kept on the shelves there in his room, so he hadn't removed anything from the office, which might have been interfering with justice.

"Was he dead when you left?" Cramer asked.

Wolfe nodded. "Yes, sir. I stayed for that."

"He's still dead." Cramer is not a wag; he was just stating a fact. He pushed his chair back an inch, wrinkling the carpet. "It was cyanide. To be verified, but it was. We found a crumpled paper on the floor under the end of the couch. Toilet paper. Not the kind in your bathroom."

"Thank you," Wolfe said drily.

"Yeah, I know. You didn't do it. You were with me. Goodwin wasn't, not all the time, but I'm willing to be realistic. There was white powder left on the paper, and when we put a drop of water on a spot it had the cyanide smell. The glass seemed to have it too, but there was the smell of the drink." He looked up at me. "Sit down, Goodwin. Do you know what the drink was?"

"No," I replied, "but O'Garro said it was Pernod. He said he saw him pour it and put it down on the table when Hansen called to him. And when—"

"Damn you," Cramer exploded, "you had the nerve to start in on them? You know damn well—"

"Nuts," I said distinctly. "I asked no questions. He volunteered it. And when Assa was here this evening just before dinner he drank Pernod—or rather, he gulped it, and said it was his drink."

"He was here? Before dinner?"

"Right. Unless Mr. Wolfe says he wasn't."

"What did he want?"

"Ask Mr. Wolfe."

"No," Wolfe said emphatically. "My brain is fuddled. Tell Mr. Cramer what Mr. Assa said and what I said. All of it."

I got a chair and sat, and shut my eyes for a moment to get my brain arranged. I had had a long and strict training, but the past hour had shoved other details to the rear, and I had to adjust. I did so, opened my eyes, and reported. When I had got to the end, with Assa saying, "Very well," and departing, I added, "That's it. If we had a tape of it I'd welcome a comparison. Any questions?"

No reply. Cramer had stuck a cigar in his mouth and was chewing on it. "Go down to the office," he said, "and get your typewriter and some paper. Tell Stebbins I said so, and take it somewhere and type that. All of it."

"That can wait," Wolfe said gruffly, "until we're through here. I want him here."

Cramer didn't press it. He took the cigar from his mouth and said, "And then you phoned me."

"Yes. As soon as Mr. Assa was out of the house."

"Too bad you didn't tell me what had happened. Assa would still be alive."

"Perhaps."

Cramer goggled. "By God, you admit it?"

"I'll admit anything you please. I have had cause for chagrin before now, Mr. Cramer, but nothing to compare with this. I didn't know that mortification could cut so deeply. One more stab and it would have got the bone. If Mr. Assa had had the wallet in his possession, actually on his person—then it would have been consummate. That would have finished me."

"He did."

"He did what?"

"He had the wallet. In his breast pocket. It has been identified as the one Dahlmann was carrying—sufficiently identified. There was no paper in it containing the answers."

Wolfe swallowed. He swallowed again. "I am humiliated beyond expression, Mr. Cramer. Go and get the murderer. But lock me in here; I would only botch it for you. The rest of the house is yours."

Cramer and I regarded him, not with pity. We both knew him too well. Naturally he was bitter, since he had got the stage all set for one of his major performances, with him as the star, and had actually started his act, only to have a prominent member of the cast, presumably the villain, up and die on him, there before his eyes. It was certainly upsetting, but neither Cramer nor I was sap enough to believe that he was humiliated beyond expression—or anything else beyond expression.

Cramer didn't go to pat his shoulder. He merely asked, "What if he wasn't murdered? What if he dosed his drink himself?"

"Pfui," Wolfe said, and I lifted a hand to hide a grin. He went on, "If he did, he had the paper of cyanide in his pocket when he left wherever he was to come here. With a choice of places for ending his life, I refuse to believe he selected the audience he knew he would have in my office—and with that wallet in his pocket."

"Something might have happened after he got here."

"I don't believe it. He had had ample opportunity to talk with his associates beforehand."

124

"He might have wanted to throw suspicion on someone."

"Then for an intelligent man he was remarkably clumsy about it. Unless you have details unknown to me?"

"No. I think he was murdered." Cramer dumped that by turning his hand over. "If I understand you, after he came and tried to get you to call off the meeting, you assumed he had killed Dahlmann and taken the wallet, and you intended to screw it out of him tonight. Was that it?"

"No, sir. You forget that I was not interested in the murder. I assumed, of course, that points relevant to the murder would be broached, and that was why I invited you to come. I also assumed that Assa had taken the wallet, because—"

"Sure you did," Cramer blurted. "Naturally. Because he was certain you had sent the answers to the contestants, so he knew nobody else could have sent them, and the only way he could have known that was obvious."

"Nothing of the sort." Wolfe didn't sound humiliated, but I'm not saying he hadn't been. It was just that he had a good repair department. "On the contrary. Because he was eager to give me the credit for sending the answers, though he knew I hadn't. If he hadn't known who had sent them he wouldn't have risked such a move, so he had sent them himself, getting them from the paper in Dahlmann's wallet. I rejected the remote possibility that he had got them from the originals in the safe deposit vault, since he wouldn't have dared go there alone and ask for that box. The brilliant stroke that saved the contest, for which he heaped praise on me, was his own. Therefore he had either taken the wallet himself or he knew who had, and the former was the more probable, since he said he had come to me on his own initiative and responsibility without consulting his associates. And of course he wanted the meeting canceled."

"Why not?" Cramer demanded. "Why didn't you cancel it?"

"Because I had a double obligation, and not to him. One was my obligation to my client, the firm of Lippert, Buff and Assa, to do the job I had been hired for, and the other was my obligation to myself, not to be hoodwinked." He stopped short, tightened his lips, and half closed his eyes. "Not to be hoodwinked," he said bitterly, "and look at me."

He opened his eyes. "Hoodwinked, however, not by a Mr. Assa trying to save a perfume contest, but by a man who had already murdered once and was ready to murder again. I was assuming that Assa had taken Dahlmann's wallet, but not that he had killed him; and anyway, that was your affair. Now it's quite different. To assume that Assa was killed merely because someone knew he had taken the wallet and sent the answers to the contestants would be infantile. To assume that Assa knew that Hansen or Buff or O'Garro or Heery had taken the wallet and sent the answers, and that one of them killed him to forestall disclosure, would be witless. The only tolerable assumption is that Assa knew, or had reason to believe, that one of them had killed Dahlmann. That would be worth killing for, but by heaven, not in my office!"

"Yeah, that was cheeky." Cramer took the cigar from his mouth, what was left of it. "Why just those four? What about the contestants?"

"Nonsense. Not worth considering. Send them home. Can you possibly think them worth discussing?"

"No," Cramer conceded, "but I'm not sending them home. They were there when the poison was put in the drink. They're being questioned now, separately. I thought you wouldn't mind if we used the rooms on that floor and the basement."

"I am in no position to mind anything whatever." It *had* cut deep. "I respect your routine, Mr. Cramer, question them by all means, but I doubt if he was inept enough to let himself be observed. Also you may get more than you want. Miss Frazee may well declare that she saw each of them in turn, including the other contestants, putting something into his drink. I advise you not to let her know that the paper was found. —By the way. You told me last Wednesday that none of those five men—you were including Assa—could prove he hadn't gone to Dahlmann's place the night he was killed. Does that still hold?"

"Yes. Why?"

"I wanted to know."

"What for? You looking for a murderer now? By God, I *could* lock you in!"

"I still have my job, to find out who took the wallet.

126

Those who may suppose I'll now be satisfied that Mr. Assa took it will be wrong." All of a sudden, with no warning, Wolfe blew. He opened his mouth and roared, "Confound it, can a man kill with impunity in my office, with my liquor in my glass?"

"A goddam shame," Cramer said. "But you stick to your job and let mine alone. I'd hate to see you humiliated again. I wouldn't mind humiliating you myself some day, but not by a stranger and a murderer. Anyway, if it's down to those four, two of them are your clients."

"No. My client is a business firm."

"Okay, but keep off. I don't like the look on your face, but I seldom do. Other things I don't like. You seem positive the contestants are out of it."

"I am."

"Why? What do you know that you haven't told me?"

"Nothing of any substance."

"Do you know of any motive any of those four men had for killing Dahlmann?"

"No. Only that apparently they all envied him. Do you know of any?"

"None that has looked good enough. Now we'll look closer. Have you any information at all that points in any way to one of them?"

"No one more than another."

"If you get any I want it. You keep off. Another thing I don't like, this client stuff. I have known you—come in!"

Bad manners again. It wasn't his door that was knocked on. It opened and a dick stepped in.

"Inspector, the lieutenant wants you. He's in the kitchen with one of the women."

Cramer said he'd be right down, and arose. The dick left. Cramer addressed me. "Get your machine and type that talk with Assa. Bring it up and do it here so you can keep an eye on your boss. We don't want him humiliated again." He walked out.

I faced Wolfe and he faced me. I wouldn't have liked his look either if his expression of cold fury had been meant for me. "Any instructions?" I asked.

"Not at present. I may call on you any time during the night. I won't try to sleep. With a murderer roaming my house, and me empty-handed and empty-headed . . ."

"He's not roaming. You ought to squeeze in a nap,

with your door locked of course. I'll stick around until the company leaves—and incidentally, what about refreshments? With the gate-crashers there won't be enough marinated mushrooms and almond balls. Sandwiches and coffee?"

"Yes." He shut his eyes. "Archie. Let me alone."

"Glad to."

I left him and went downstairs. Opening the door to the kitchen to tell Fritz sandwiches and coffee, I saw only Cramer and Rowcliff and Susan Tescher and Hibbard, and backed out. Three guests in uniform were in the hall, one in charge of the front door. The doors to the dining room and front room were closed. The one to the office was also closed, and I opened it and entered. The corpse was gone. Half a dozen scientists were still researching, and Purley Stebbins and a dick from the DA's office had Patrick O'Garro between them over by the refreshment table. That could last all night, bringing each one in separately to tell who was where and when. Fritz was still perched behind Wolfe's desk and I went to him.

"Nice party."

"It's nothing to joke about, Archie. *Cochon!*"

"I never joke. I'm relieving you. Evidently nothing in this room is available, including the refreshments, so I guess you'll have to produce sandwiches and coffee. You'll find characters in the kitchen, but ignore them. If they complain tell them you're under orders. Don't bother taking anything up to Mr. Wolfe. He's chewing nails and doesn't want to be disturbed."

Fritz said he should have some beer, and I said okay if he wanted to risk it, and he departed. As for me, I was relieving Fritz on guard duty, and furthermore, the day had not come for me to tell Purley that Cramer had ordered me to remove my typewriter to another room and would he kindly permit me to do so; and I didn't want to lug it up two flights anyway; and it would be interesting and instructive to watch trained detectives solving a crime.

Speaking of trained detectives, I was supposed to be one, but I certainly wasn't bragging. I went to my desk and took my gun from the holster and put it in the drawer, and locked the drawer. In this report I could have omitted any mention of it, but I didn't want to fudge, and I preferred not to skip the way I felt when, after going around armed for several days, I thoughtfully set it up for a homicide right there in the office—and a lot of good my gun did. To hell with it. It would have made it perfect if, soon after ditching it, I had really needed it, but I didn't get even that satisfaction.

I got paper and carbon from another drawer, rolled the typewriter stand around to the rear of Wolfe's desk, sat in Wolfe's chair, and started tapping.

20

I would appreciate it if they would call a halt on all their devoted efforts to find a way to abolish war or eliminate disease or run trains with atoms or extend the span of human life to a couple of centuries, and everybody concentrate for a while on how to wake me up in the morning without my resenting it. It may be that a bevy of beautiful maidens in pure silk yellow very sheer gowns, barefooted, singing *Oh, What a Beautiful Morning* and scattering rose petals over me would do the trick, but I'd have to try it.

That Tuesday morning it was terrible. I had been in bed only three hours, and what woke me was the phone, about the worst way of all. I rolled over, opened my eyes to see the alarm clock at seven-twenty-five, reached, and yanked the damn thing off the cradle.

"Yeah?"

"Good morning, Archie. Can you be down in thirty minutes? I'm breakfasting with Saul, Fred, Orrie, and Bill."

That woke me all right, though it had no effect on the resentment. I told Wolfe I'd try, rolled out, and headed for the bathroom. Usually I yawn around for a couple of minutes before digging in, but there wasn't time. As I shaved I wished I had asked him what kind of a program it was, so I would know what to dress for, but if it had been anything special he would have said so, and I just grabbed the shirt on top.

When I made it to the ground floor, in thirty minutes flat, they were in the dining room with coffee. As I greeted them Fritz came with my orange juice, and I sat and took a healthy swallow.

"This is a hell of a time," I said, still resenting, "to spring a surprise party on me."

Bill Gore laughed. I said something funny to him once back in 1948, and ever since he has had a policy of laughing whenever I open my trap. Bill is not too smart to live, but he's tough and hangs on. Orrie Cather is smarter and is not ashamed of it, and since he got rid of the idea that it would be a good plan for him to take over my job, some years ago, he has helped Wolfe with some very neat errands when called upon. Fred Durkin is just Fred Durkin and knows it. He thinks Wolfe could prove who killed Cock Robin any time he felt like spending half an hour on it. He thinks Wolfe could prove anything whatever. You've met Saul Panzer, the one and only.

As I finished my orange juice and started on griddle cakes, Wolfe expounded. He said the surprise was incidental; he had phoned them after I had gone to bed, when he had conceived a procedure.

"Fine," I approved, spreading butter to melt, "we've got a procedure. For these gentlemen?"

"For all of us," he said. "I have described the situation to them, as much as they'll need. It is a procedure of desperation, with perhaps one chance in twenty of success. After hours on it, most of the night, this was the best I could do. As you know, I was assuming that one of four men—Hansen, Buff, O'Garro, Heery—had killed Dahlmann and taken the wallet, and that because Assa had learned of it or suspected it he had been killed too."

"I know that's what you told Cramer."

"It's also what I told myself."

"Why would one of them kill Dahlmann?"

"I don't know, but if he did he had a reason. That remains, along with his identity. To search into motives would take long and toilsome investigation, and even then motive alone is nothing. I preferred to focus on identity. Which of the four? I went over and over every word they have uttered, to you and to me; all their tones and glances and postures. There was no hint—at least, not for me. I considered all possible lines of inquiry, and found

130

that all of them either had already been pursued by the police, or were now being pursued, or were hopelessly tenuous. All I had left, at five o'clock this morning, that gave the slightest promise of some result without a prolonged and laborious siege, was the possibility of a satisfactory answer to the question: where did he get the poison?"

Chewing griddle cake and ham, I looked at him. "Good lord, if that's the best we can do. Cramer has an army on it right now. There are six of us and we have no badges, and if—" I stopped because I saw his eyes. "You've got something?"

"Yes. A straw to grab at. Can't it be reasonably supposed that the decision to kill Mr. Assa was made only yesterday afternoon, resulting from the situation caused by the contestants' receipt of the answers by mail? Various circumstances support such—"

"Don't bother. I've gone over it too a little. I'll buy that."

"Then some time yesterday afternoon, not before, he decided that Mr. Assa would have to be killed, and he conceived the idea of using cyanide and putting it in his drink. Correct?"

"Yes."

"Then where the devil did he get the cyanide?"

"I couldn't—oh. That does make it a little special."

"It does indeed. Did he choose cyanide as something he knew to be lightning-swift and go out and buy some? Hardly. He could of course have procured it easily—a photographic supply house, for one—but he was not an imbecile. No. He knew where some was, handy; he knew where he could get some without being observed. Where? There are a thousand possibilities, and it may have been any one of them, but I didn't bother speculating about them because one of them was looking at me—or rather, at you. I hadn't seen it, but you had."

"Hold it." I put my coffee cup down. "I've seen it?"

"Yes."

"And told you about it?"

"Yes."

"That's interesting." I closed my eyes, opened them, and slapped the table. "Oh, sure. The display cases at the LBA office. I might have thought of it myself if I had stayed up all night—but I don't remember seeing any cyanide."

"You weren't looking for it. You said there are thousands of items from hundreds of firms. We're going to look for it."

"After it's gone? If he took it, it's not there."

"All the better. If he took only what he needed of it we'll find the residue. If he took it all yesterday or has removed the residue since, we'll find where it was—or we won't. There must be a list of the contents of those cases. There's no point in our trying to intrude before office hours, so there's plenty of time. Now for the details. I'll be with you, but you should know what I have in mind for the various eventualities—all of you. Fritz! Coffee!"

He gave us details.

If anyone considers this incident an exception to Wolfe's rule never to leave the house on business, I say no. It was not business. He was after the man who had abused his hospitality, which was unforgivable, and made him eat crow in front of Cramer, which was outrageous. I have evidence. On a later day, when he was going over the expense account I had prepared for LBA, he left in the fare for one taxi that morning, the one that Fred and Orrie and Bill took, but took out the other, the one that had carried him and Saul and me.

It lacked a minute of nine-thirty when the six of us entered an elevator in the modern midtown skyscraper, but when we got out at the twenty-second floor the aristocratic brunette with nice little ears was there on the job behind her eight-foot desk. The sudden appearance of a gang of half a dozen males startled her a little, but as I approached and she recognized me she recovered.

I told her good morning. "I'm afraid we'll be making a little disturbance, but we've got a job to do. This is Mr. Nero Wolfe."

Wolfe, at my elbow, nodded. "We have to inventory the contents of the cabinets. The death of Mr. Assa—of course you know of it."

"Yes, I . . . I know."

"That makes it necessary to proceed without delay."

She looked beyond us, and I turned to do likewise. The squad was certainly proceeding without delay. Saul Panzer had slid open the glass front of the end cabinet at the

132

left wall and had his notebook out. Fred Durkin was at the end cabinet at the right wall, and Bill and Orrie were at the far wall, which was solid with cabinets, a stretch of some fifty feet. It was a relief to see that they all had doors open. I had seen no locks on my former visit, but there could have been tricky ones. We had brought along an assortment of keys, but using them would have made it complicated.

"I know nothing about this," the brunette said. "Who told you to do it?"

"It's part of a job," Wolfe told her, "that was given me by Messers Buff, O'Garro, and Assa last Wednesday. I refer you to them. —Come, Archie."

We headed for the cabinets at the right wall, those nearest the elevators, and as we reached them Fred left and went to join Saul at the left wall. That was according to the plan of battle as outlined at headquarters. I didn't bother to get out my notebook, wanting both hands free for moving things when necessary. For the first cabinet it wasn't necessary. It held a picture of an ocean liner, some miniature bags of a line of fertilizers, cartons of cigarettes, a vacuum cleaner, and various other items. The bottom shelf of the second cabinet was no more promising, with an outboard motor, soaps and detergents, canned soup, and beer in both bottles and cans, but the second shelf had packaged goods and got more attention. It didn't seem likely that cyanide would have fitted in with cereals and cake mixes and noodles, but the program said to look at each and every package. I was doing so, with Wolfe standing behind me, when an authoritative voice sounded.

"Are you Nero Wolfe? What's going on?"

I straightened and turned. A six-foot executive with a jutting jaw was facing Wolfe and wanted no nonsense. Since he hadn't emerged from an elevator, he must have been inside and the brunette had summoned him.

"I've explained," Wolfe said, "to the woman at the desk."

"I know what you told her and it sounds fishy. Get away from these cabinets and stay away until I can check."

Wolfe shook his head. "I'm sorry, Mr. . . ."

"My name's Falk."

"I'm sorry we can't oblige you, Mr. Falk. I was hired by Mr. Buff and Mr. O'Garro—and Mr. Assa, who is dead. We've started and we're going to finish. You look truculent, but I advise you to consult Mr. Buff or Mr. O'Garro. Where are they?"

"They're not here."

"You must know where they are. Phone them."

"I'm going to, and you're going to stay away from these cabinets until I do."

"No, sir." Wolfe was firm but unruffled. "I make allowances for your state of mind, Mr. Falk, after what happened last night, but you must know I'm not a bandit and these men are working for me. It shouldn't take long to get Mr. Buff or Mr. O'Garro. Do so by all means."

One test of a good executive is how long it takes him to realize he has lost an argument, and Falk passed it. He turned on his heel and left, striding across the carpet to the door leading to the inside corridor. Wolfe and I resumed, finishing with the shelf of packages and going on to the next one—buckets and cans of paint, electric irons, and so forth.

During the next half hour the elevators delivered eight or nine people, not more than that, and took most of them away again, but nobody bothered us. On the whole it was a nice quiet place to work. Once Wolfe and I thought we might be getting hot, when we came to the display of Jonas Hibben & Co., Pharmaceuticals, but it seemed to be intact, with no vacant spot, and there was no box or bottle from which someone could have removed a dose of cyanide. We gave it up finally, and moved on, and were at the last cabinet on that wall when Saul called to us to come and look at something, and we crossed the room to him, where he and Fred were focusing on the second shelf of the last cabinet in their battery.

The dignified little card—they were all dignified and little—identified it as the exhibit of the Allcoran Laboratories, Inc. There were a couple of dozen boxes, small and large, with the small ones in front and the large ones in the rear, and three rows of brown bottles, all the same size, I would say about a pint.

Saul said, "Middle row, fourth bottle from the left. You have to tip the one in front to see the label."

Wolfe stepped closer. Instead of tipping the one in front he lifted it with a thumb and forefinger, to get a clear view, and I got one too over his shoulder. No squinting was required. At the top of the label was printed in black, in large type, KCN. At the bottom was printed in red, also in large type, POISON. In between, and below the POISON there was some stuff in smaller type, but I didn't strain to get it. The bottle was so dark it would have to be lifted out and held up to the light for a look at the contents, and that wouldn't do, but you could see there was something white in it, almost up to the neck.

"Today's daily double," I said. "It was here, and we found it."

Wolfe returned the bottle he had lifted, gently and carefully. "Did you touch it?" he asked Saul. He knew darned well he hadn't, since our orders had been not to touch anything until we knew what it was, or at least that it wasn't what we were looking for. Saul said no, and Wolfe called to Bill and Orrie to come and bring chairs along, and Saul and Fred also went and got chairs. They lined the four chairs up in a row in front of the cabinet, their backs to it, and the quartet sat, facing the room and the elevators. They looked pretty impressive that way, the four of them, and no bottle of poison was ever better guarded.

That was the sight that met four pairs of eyes when Oliver Buff, Patrick O'Garro, Rudolph Hansen, and Talbot Heery stepped from an elevator into the reception room.

"Good morning, gentlemen!" Wolfe sang out, in about as nasty a tone as I had ever known him to use.

They headed for us.

21

It rarely gets you anywhere, practically never, but you always do it. When four men enter a room and one of them sees six men grouped in front of a cabinet which has in it a bottle of poison out of which he has recently shaken a spoonful onto a piece of toilet paper, to be used for killing a man, you try to watch all their faces like a hawk for some sign of which one it is. That time it was more useless than usual. They had all had a hard and probably sleepless night, and maybe hadn't been to bed at all. They looked it, and certainly none of them liked what he saw. Three of them—Buff, O'Garro, and Hansen —all spoke at once. They wanted to know who and what and why and when, oblivious of the presence of a customer who was seated across the room.

Wolfe was incisive. "It would be better, I think, to retire somewhere. This is rather public."

"Who are these men?" Buff demanded.

"They are working for the firm of Lippert, Buff and Assa, through me. They are now—"

"Get them out of here!"

"No. They're guarding an object in that cabinet. I intend shortly to tell the police to come and get the object, and meanwhile these four men will stay. They're all armed, so I—"

"Why, goddam you—" O'Garro blurted, but Hansen gripped his arm and said, "Let's go inside," and turned him around. Buff seemed about to choke, but controlled it, and led the way, with his partner and lawyer following, then Heery, then Wolfe, and then me. As I passed through the door to the corridor I turned for a glance at the four sentries, and Orrie winked at me.

The executive committee room was much more presentable than it had been before, with everything in order. The second the door was shut O'Garro started yapping, but Hansen got his arm again and steered him around to a chair at the far side of the big table, and took one there himself, so they had the windows back of them. Wolfe and I took the near side, with Heery at one end, on Wolfe's left, and Buff at the other, on my right.

"What's this object in a cabinet?" O'Garro demanded as Wolfe sat. "What are you trying to pull?"

"It will be better," Wolfe said, "if you let me describe the situation. Then we can—"

"We know the situation," Hansen put in. "We want to know what you think you're doing."

"That's simple. I'm preparing to learn which of you four men killed Louis Dahlmann, and took the wallet, and killed Vernon Assa."

Three of them stared. Heery said, "Jesus. Is that simple?"

Hansen said, "I advise you, Mr. Wolfe, to choose your words—and also your acts. With more care. This could cost you your license and much of your reputation, and possibly more. Let's have the facts. What is the object in the cabinet?"

"A bottle of cyanide of potassium, in the display of All-coran Laboratories, with the cap seal broken and almost certainly some of the contents removed. That can be determined."

"There in that cabinet?" Hansen couldn't believe it.

"Yes, sir."

"A deadly poison there on public display?"

"Oh, come, Mr. Hansen. Don't feign an ignorance you can't possibly own. Dozens of deadly poisons are available to the public at thousands of counters, including cyanide with its many uses. You must know that, but if you want it on the record that you were astonished by my announcement you have witnesses. Shall I ask the others if they were astonished too?"

"No. —I advise you, Oliver, and you too, Pat, to say nothing whatever and answer no questions. This man is treacherous."

Wolfe skipped the tribute. "That will expedite matters," he said approvingly. His eyes moved. "I must tell the police about that bottle of poison reasonably soon, so the less I'm interrupted the better, but if you all refuse to say anything whatever I'll be wasting my time and might as well phone them now. There are one or two things I should know—for example, can I narrow it down? Of course Mr. Buff and Mr. O'Garro were on these premises yesterday afternoon. Were you, Mr. Hansen?"

"Yes."

"When?"

"Roughly, from four o'clock until after six."

"Were you, Mr. Heery?"

"I was here twice. I stopped in for a few minutes when I went to lunch, and around four-thirty I was here for half an hour."

"That's too bad." Wolfe put his palms on the table. "Now, gentlemen, I'll be as brief as may be. When I'm through we can consider whether I have to enter a defense against Mr. Hansen's charge of treachery. Until the moment of Mr. Assa's collapse in my office last evening I was concerned only with the job I had been hired for, not with murder. I invited Mr. Cramer to the meeting because I expected that developments to be contrived by me would remove both the contestants and yourselves as primary targets of his inquiry, which was surely desirable. My first objective was to demonstrate to the contestants that their receipt of the answers by mail had made it impossible to proceed with the verses that had been given them last week, and it would be futile for them to resist the inevitable; and to get their unanimous agreement to the distribution of new verses as soon as their freedom of movement was restored."

"You say that now." Hansen was buying nothing.

"It will be supported. I was confident I could do that, for they had no feasible alternative. Then I would be through with them and they would leave, and I would pursue the second objective with the rest of you. I confess that the second objective was not at all clear, and the path to it was poorly mapped, until nearly seven o'clock last evening, when Mr. Assa called. —Mr. Hansen, did you know that Mr. Assa came to see me at that hour yesterday?"

"No. I don't know it now."

"Did you, Mr. Buff?"

"No."

"Mr. O'Garro?"

"No!"

"Mr. Heery?"

"I did not."

Wolfe nodded. "One of you is lying, and that may help. He came and we talked. Mr. Goodwin was present, and he has typed a transcript of the conversation for Mr. Cramer. He could report it to you now, but it would take too long, so I'll summarize it. Mr. Assa said he was speaking for himself, not for the firm; that he had not consulted his associates. He congratulated me for what he called my brilliant stroke in sending the answers to the contestants and thereby rescuing the contest from ruin. He offered his personal guarantee for payment of my fee. He took a drink of Pernod and poured another. And he began and ended with a demand that I call off the meeting for last evening. As for me, I denied sending the answers to the contestants, and I refused to call off the meeting. He left in a huff."

Wolfe took a breath. "That was all I needed. Mr. Assa's pretended certainty that I had sent the answers, and his eagerness to give me credit for it privately, could only mean that he had sent them himself, having got them from the paper in Dahlmann's wallet, or that he knew who had. The former was much more probable. Now the second objective of the meeting, and the path to it, were quite clear. I would proceed as planned with the contestants, get their consent to a new agreement, and then dismiss them. After they had gone I would tackle Mr. Assa and the rest of you, in the presence of Mr. Cramer. I wasn't assuming that Assa had killed Dahlmann; on the contrary, I was assuming that he hadn't, since in that case he would hardly have dared expose himself as he did in coming to me. My supposition was that Assa had gone to Dahlmann's apartment, found him dead, and took the wallet—one of Mr. Cramer's theories, as you know. If so, it had to be disclosed to Mr. Cramer, and the sooner the better—the better not only for the demands of justice, but for my client, the firm of Lippert, Buff and Assa. It would embarrass an individual, Vernon Assa, but it would be to the advantage of everyone else. It would eliminate the contestants as murder suspects, and would substantially lessen the burden of suspicion for the rest of you. I intended to expound that position to all of you and get you to help me exert pressure on Mr. Assa, and I expected to succeed."

He took another deep breath, deeper. "I am, as you see, confessing to an egregious blunder. It came from my failure to consider sufficiently the possibility that Mr. Assa had himself been duped or had miscalculated. I now condemn myself, but on the other hand, if I had known at nine o'clock last evening exactly what—"

"You can omit the if's," Hansen said coldly. "Apologize to yourself, we're not interested. How did Assa miscalculate?"

"By thinking that the man who had admitted to him that he had taken Dahlmann's wallet was telling the truth when he said that he had found Dahlmann dead. By dismissing the possibility that in fact he had killed Dahlmann."

"Wait a minute," Heery objected. "You thought that yourself about Assa."

"But Assa had come to me, and besides, I have said I blundered. It was painfully obvious, of course, when Assa died before my eyes. No effort was required to learn what had happened; the only question was, which one of you had made it happen. Which one—"

"Not obvious to me," O'Garro said.

"Then I'll describe it." Wolfe shifted in the chair, which was almost big enough but not used to him. "Since that bottle is under guard, with great assurance. Yesterday afternoon Assa learned somehow that one of you had Dahlmann's wallet in your possession. Whether he learned it by chance or by enterprise doesn't matter; he learned it, and he confronted you. You—"

Heery put in, "You just said that you assumed Assa took the wallet from Dahlmann himself. And he had it in his pocket."

"Pfui." Wolfe was getting testy. "If Assa took it, who killed him and what for? His death changed everything, including my assumptions. He confronted one of you with his knowledge that you had the wallet. You explained that you had gone to Dahlmann's apartment that night, found him dead, and took the wallet, and Assa believed you. Either you told him that you had sent the answers to the contestants, or that you hadn't. If the former, Assa conceived the stratagem of giving me credit for it as a blind; if the latter, he really thought I had done it. You two discussed the situation and decided what to do, or perhaps you didn't; Assa may have discussed it only with himself and made his own plans. It would be interesting to know whether he insisted on keeping the wallet or you insisted on his taking it. If I knew that I would have a better guess who you are."

Wolfe's tone sharpened. "Whether or not you knew of his visit to me beforehand, you knew its result. He told you that I had refused to cancel the meeting, and that both of you would of course have to come. This raises an interesting point. If it was his report of his talk with me that so heightened your alarm that you decided to kill him, then you went to the cabinet to get the poison after seven o'clock. If your fatal resolve was formed earlier, before he came to me, you might have gone to the cabinet

140

earlier. The former seems more likely. Dread feeds on itself. At first you were satisfied that Assa believed you, that he had no slight suspicion that you had killed Dahlmann, but that sort of satisfaction is infested with cancer —the cancer of mortal fear. The fear that Assa might himself suspect you, or already did; the fear that if he didn't suspect you, I would; the fear that if I didn't suspect you, the police would. When Assa told you of his failure to persuade me to cancel the meeting, the fear became terror; though you believed him when he said that he had given me no hint of his knowledge regarding the wallet, there was no telling what he would do or say under pressure from me with the others present. As I said, it seems likely that it was then, when fear had festered into the panic of terror, that you resolved to kill him. Therefore it—"

"This is drivel," Hansen said curtly. "Pure speculation. If you have a fact, what is it?"

"Out there, Mr. Hansen." Wolfe aimed a thumb over his shoulder at the door. "It could even be conclusive if that bottle has identifiable fingerprints, but I doubt if you —one of you—had lost his mind utterly. That's my fact, and it justifies a question. Mr. Assa left my office yesterday at ten minutes past seven. Who was on these premises later than that? Were you, Mr. Hansen?"

"No. I told you. I was here from four o'clock on, but left before six-thirty."

"Were you, Mr. Heery?"

"No. I told you when I was here."

"Mr. O'Garro?"

"Don't answer, Pat," Hansen commanded him.

"Pah." Wolfe was disgusted. "Something so easy to explore? If you prefer the plague—"

"I prefer," O'Garro said, "to have this out with you here and now." His bluster was gone. He was being very careful and keeping his eyes straight at Wolfe. "I was here all yesterday afternoon. I saw Assa and spoke with him several times, but always with others present. Buff and I left together around half-past seven and met Assa at a restaurant. We ate something and went from there to your place—Buff and I did. Assa stopped off for an errand and came on alone."

"What was his errand?"

"I don't know. He didn't say."

"At the restaurant, what did he say about his visit to me?"

"Nothing. He didn't mention it. The first I heard of it was here from you."

"When did you make the appointment to meet him at the restaurant?"

"I didn't make it."

"Who did?"

O'Garro's jaw worked. His eyes hadn't left Wolfe. "I'll reserve that," he said.

"You preferred," Wolfe reminded him, "to have it out here and now."

"That will do," Hansen said, with authority. "As your counsel, Pat, I instruct you, and you too, Oliver, to answer no more questions. I said this man is treacherous and I repeat it. He was in your employ in a confidential capacity, and he is trying to put you in jeopardy on a capital charge. Don't answer him. —If you have anything else to say, Wolfe, we're listening."

Wolfe ignored him and looked at Buff. "Fortunately, Mr. Buff, Mr. O'Garro has spared me the effort of persuading you to disobey your attorney, since he has told me that you left here with him around seven-thirty." His eyes moved. "I deny that I am treacherous. My client is a business entity called Lippert, Buff and Assa. Until the moment of Mr. Assa's death I devoted myself exclusively to my client's interests by working on the job that had been given me. Indeed, I am still doing so, but the circumstances have altered. The question is, what will best serve the interests of that business entity under these new circumstances? Its corollary is, how can I finish my job and learn who took the wallet without exposing the murderer? I can't."

He flattened his palms on the desk. "Mr. Dahlmann, who was apparently equipped to furnish the vitality and vigor formerly supplied by Mr. Lippert, has been killed—by one of you. Mr. Assa, who rashly incurred great personal risk for the sake of the firm, has also been killed—by one of you. Who, then, is the traitor? Who has reduced the firm to a strait from which it may never recover? If it is reasonable for you to expect me to regard my client's interests as paramount, as it is, it is equally reasonable

142

or me to expect you to do the same; and you are simple-ons if you don't see that those interests demand the ex-posure of the murderer as quickly and surely as possible."

His eyes fixed on the lawyer. "Mr. Hansen. You are counsel for the firm of Lippert, Buff and Assa?"

"I am."

"Are you Mr. Buff's personal attorney?"

"Of record? No."

"Or Mr. O'Garro's?"

"No."

"Then I charge you with treachery to your client. I assert that you betray your client's vital interests when you instruct these men to withhold answers to my ques-tions. —No no, don't bother to reply. Draft a twenty-page brief tomorrow at your leisure." He left him for the mem-bers of the firm. "I have noted that you have not raised the question of motive. I myself have not broached it be-cause I know little or nothing about it—that is, the motive for killing Dahlmann. Mr. Cramer of course has a stack of them, good, bad, and indifferent. I have nothing at all for Mr. Hansen and next to nothing for Mr. Heery, and anyway the timetable shelves them tentatively. For Mr. O'Garro, nothing. For Mr. Buff, nothing conclusive, but material for speculation. I have gathered that he more or less inherited his eminence in the firm on the death of Mr. Lippert, who had trained him; that since Mr. Lippert's death he has gloried in his status of senior partner and clung to it tenaciously; that his abilities are negligible ex-cept for one narrow field; and that there was a widespread expectation that before long Mr. Dahlmann would become the master instead of the servant. I don't know how severely that prospect galled Mr. Buff, but you must know." He focused on the senior partner. "Especially you, Mr. Buff. Would you care to tell me?"

Buff darted a glance at Hansen, but the lawyer had no instructions, and he went to Wolfe. His round red face was puffy and flabby, and a strand of his white hair, dangling over his brow, had been annoying me and I had been tempted to tell him to brush it back. Around the corner at the end of the table, at my right, he was close enough for me to do it myself.

He wasn't indignant. He was a big man and an im-portant man, and this was a very serious matter. "Your attempt to give me a motive," he told Wolfe, "is not very successful. We all resented Dahlmann a little. He got on our nerves. I think some of us hated him—for instance, O'Garro here. O'Garro always did hate him. But in trying to give me a motive you're overlooking something. If I killed him to keep him from crowding me out at LBA, I must have been crazy, because why did I take the wallet? Taking the wallet was what got LBA into these grave difficulties. Was I crazy?"

"By no means." Wolfe met his eyes. "You may have gone there merely to get the wallet, and took the gun along because you were determined to get it, and the opportunity to get rid of him became irresistible after you were with him. Leaving, you would certainly take the wallet. That was what you had gone for; and in any case, you didn't want it found on his body with that paper in it. You were not in a state of mind to consider calmly the consequences of your taking it. By the way, what have you done with the paper? It must have been in the wallet, since you sent the answers to the contestants."

"That's going too far, Wolfe." Buff's voice raised a little. "You only suggested a motive, but now you're accusing me. With witnesses here, don't forget that. But what you said about the vital interests of this firm, that they are paramount, that made sense and I agree with you. At a time like this personal considerations are of no account. So I must tell you of a little mistake O'Garro made—I don't say he did it deliberately, it may have slipped his mind that he did make the appointment for us to meet Assa at the restaurant. He was in his office, and he came to my office and said that Assa had phoned and he had arranged for us to meet him at Grainger's at a quarter to eight."

I thought O'Garro was going to plug him, and O'Garro thought so too. He was across from me, at Buff's right, and he was out of his chair, his eyes blazing, with two fists ready, but he didn't swing. He put his fists on the table and leaned on them, toward Buff, until his face was only a foot away from the senior partner's.

"You're too old to hit," he said, grinding it out between his teeth. "Too old and too goddam dirty. You said I hated Dahlmann. Maybe I didn't love him, but I didn't hate him. You did. Seeing him coming up on his way to

ke over and boot you out—no wonder you hated him
—and by God, I felt sorry for you!"

O'Garro straightened up and looked at us. "I felt sorry
or him, gentlemen. That's how clever I was. I felt sorry
or him." He looked at Wolfe. "You asked me who made
ie appointment with Assa and I said I'd reserve it. Buff
iade it, and came to my room and told me. Any more
uestions?"

"One or two for Mr. Buff." Wolfe regarded him with
alf-closed eyes. "Mr. Buff. When were you alone with
Ir. Assa yesterday afternoon, and where and for how
ong?"

"I refuse to answer." Buff was having trouble with his
oice. "I decline to answer on advice of counsel."

"Who is your counsel?"

"Rudolph Hansen."

"He says he isn't." Wolfe's eyes moved. "Mr. Hansen?
re you now counsel for Mr. Buff?"

"No." It sounded final. "As it stands now I couldn't be
ven if I wanted to, because of a possible conflict of
iterest. His attorney is named Arnold Duffen, with an
ffice a few blocks from here."

Buff looked at him. The round red face was puffier.
Arnold may not be immediately available, Rudolph. I
rant to consult you privately. Now."

"No. Impossible."

"Then I must try to get him." Buff was leaving his
hair. "Not here. From my room."

I stopped him by taking his arm. He was going to pull
way, but I don't take a murderer's arm the way I do a
ymph's, and he ended back in his chair. I released him,
ut got up and stood beside him.

"I wish," Wolfe said, "to extend you gentlemen all
ossible courtesy, but I must transfer the responsibility
or that bottle of poison as soon as may be. Need I wait
onger?"

For three seconds no one spoke, and then O'Garro said,
Use the phone on your left."

145

22

The most important result from the standpoint of th
People of the State of New York came a couple o
months later, in June, when Oliver Buff was tried and con
victed of the first degree murder of Vernon Assa, Crame
and the DA's office having collected a batch of evidenc
which did, after all, include one good fingerprint from th
KCN bottle. But from our standpoint the most importan
result came much earlier, in fact the very next day, whe
Rudolph Hansen phoned after lunch and made a date fo
him and O'Garro and Heery to see Wolfe at six o'clocl
They came right on the dot, just as Wolfe got down fron
the plant rooms. When I took them to the office I sa
that O'Garro got the red leather chair, thinking he rate
it as the surviving partner. Probably his name would no
go into the firm's title. They sure needed some new one

They still looked as if they could use some sleep, sa
about a week, but at least they had their hair combe
They were gloomy but polite. After some recent develop
ments had been mentioned, such as a statement by Buff
secretary that on Monday afternoon she had seen Ass
in Buff's room, talking with him, with a brown wallet i
his hand, Hansen opened up. He said that in spite o
everything it would be a great relief to proceed with th
contest in a manner that would leave no loopholes fo
contention or litigation, and in connection with th
process they wanted Wolfe's help. Wolfe asked him how

"We want you to handle it," Hansen said. "We wan
you to write the verses, give them to the contestants, an
set the conditions and deadline, and, when the answer
are received, check them and award the prizes. We wan
to leave the whole thing to you. Heery refuses to let LB
handle it, and in the circumstances we can't blame him
and it's his money. You'll have full authority. There'll b
no interference from anybody. For this service LBA wi
agree to pay you fifty thousand dollars, plus expenses."

"I won't do it," Wolfe said flatly.

"Damn it, you must!" Heery rapped out.

"No, sir. I must not. I have stretched my dignity pretty thin on occasion to keep myself going, but I will not write verses for a perfume contest. That is not to impugn the dignity of any other man who may undertake it. Dignities are like faces; no two are the same. I beg you not to insist; I won't consider it. I confess that my refusal might give me a sharper twinge but for the fact that I am about to send the firm of Lippert, Buff and Assa a bill for precisely that amount—fifty thousand dollars. Plus expenses."

"What for?" Hansen was cold.

"For the job I was hired for and have completed."

"We've discussed that," O'Garro said. "We don't see it."

"You didn't do the job," Hansen said, settling it.

"No? Who did?"

"Nobody. Circumstances beyond our control and out of your control. If anybody did it, it was Buff himself, when he sent the answers to the contestants. Also Assa learning that Buff had the wallet, but the main thing was the contestants getting the answers. That was what saved the contest."

"You acknowledge that?"

"Certainly we acknowledge it. It's obvious."

"Very well. I suppose this was unavoidable." Wolfe turned. "Archie, give Mr. Hansen a dollar."

I got one out and went and proffered it, but Hansen didn't take it. "What's this?" he demanded.

"I am retaining you as my attorney, as before. I wish what I am going to tell you to have the protection of a confidential relationship between you and me. Since the interest of Mr. O'Garro and Mr. Heery runs with mine I'll trust their discretion. You may end the relationship at any moment. That's what you told me. You and I began with a privileged communication; we'll end with one."

Hansen took the dollar, not enthusiastically, and I returned to my desk. "Go ahead," he said.

"You're gouging this out of me." Wolfe was frowning. "I would have preferred to keep it to myself, but rather this than a prolonged wrangle. When you get the list of expenses accompanying my bill there will be an item on it, 'One second-hand Underwood typewriter, eighty-two dollars.' It is now at the bottom of the river, because I wanted to exclude all possibility of a slip, but I have several pages that were typed on it—or rather, I know where they are and can easily get them—and if you will secure from Inspector Cramer one of the sheets of answers that were received by the contestants, or a good facsimile, I'll arrange an opportunity for you to make a comparison. You'll find that the answers sent to the contestants were typed on the machine charged for in my expense list."

Heery burst out laughing. In the pressure of events I had forgotten what a good laugher he was, and that time he really meant it. After a few healthy roars he stopped to blurt, "You amazing sonofabitch!" and then roared some more. Hansen and O'Garro were staring, O'Garro with a deep frown, chewing at it.

When Heery had subsided enough for a normal voice to be heard Hansen spoke. "You're saying that you sent the answers to the contestants?"

"They were sent by a man in my employ. I can produce him if you insist, but I would prefer not to name him."

"I think we won't insist. Pat?"

"No." O'Garro's frown was going. "I will be damned."

"No wonder," Hansen told Wolfe, "you wanted it a privileged communication. This changes things."

"It should," Wolfe said drily. "Since you have just declared that sending the answers to the contestants saved the contest. It was to their advantage too, most of them. That was one of my objects, and the other, of course, was to spur somebody into doing something. I didn't know who or what, but I thought that would stimulate action, and it did."

"It certainly did," O'Garro agreed. "Too much action, but you couldn't help it."

"I should have helped it. Mr. Assa should be alive. I blundered." Wolfe tightened his lips. He released them. "Do you want me to get the pages that were typed on that machine for comparison?"

"No," Hansen said. "Pat?"

"No."

"But," Hansen told Wolfe, "we still want you to handle the contest. The payment will of course be in addition to the bill you're sending. It won't be—"

"No!" Wolfe bellowed, and I didn't blame him. Turning down fifty grand just once to keep your dignity in order is tough enough, and to be compelled to keep on turning it down is too much. They tried to insist, and Heery especially wouldn't let go, but finally they had to give it up. When they left and I went to the hall with them they corralled me by the rack and tried to sell me the idea of talking him into it, with some broad hints that it wouldn't cost me anything, but I gave them no hope. My mind wasn't really on their problem at all. It was on one of my own, and when I had closed the door behind them and returned to the office I tackled it without preamble.

"Okay," I told Wolfe, "it was a brilliant stroke. It was a masterpiece. It was a honey. But not only did you change the rules and tell me a direct lie, you also piled another one on by telling me that you had *not* changed the rules. How's that for a confidential relationship? Why do I ever have to believe anything you say?"

His mouth twisted. He thought he was smiling. "You can always believe me, Archie. With your memory, which is matchless, you can recall my words. I made just two categorical statements to you, when we were alone, on that matter. I said, first, *I hadn't hoped for anything as provocative as this.* That was true; I hadn't hoped for it; I was sure of it, since I had arranged it. I said, second, *I hadn't listed this among the possibilities.* That was likewise true; it wasn't a possibility, it was a certainty. I have never told you a direct lie and never will—and if I quibbled it was only to save you the necessity of telling one to Mr. Stebbins or any one else who might challenge you. Have I quoted myself correctly?"

I grunted. I couldn't very well repudiate my matchless memory.

"Are you suggesting," he demanded, "that verbal dodges are no longer to be permitted in our private conversations? By either of us?"

"No, sir."

He snorted. "You'd better not. We wouldn't last a week."

He rang for beer.

ABOUT THE AUTHOR

REX STOUT, the creator of Nero Wolfe, was born in Noblesville, Indiana, in 1886, the sixth of nine children of John and Lucetta Todhunter Stout, both Quakers. Shortly after his birth, the family moved to Wakarusa, Kansas. He was educated in a country school, but, by the age of nine, was recognized throughout the state as a prodigy in arithmetic. Mr. Stout briefly attended the University of Kansas, but left to enlist in the Navy, and spent the next two years as a warrant officer on board President Theodore Roosevelt's yacht. When he left the Navy in 1908, Rex Stout began to write freelance articles, worked as a sightseeing guide and as an itinerant bookkeeper. Later he devised and implemented a school banking system which was installed in four hundred cities and towns throughout the country. In 1927 Mr. Stout retired from the world of finance and, with the proceeds of his banking scheme, left for Paris to write serious fiction. He wrote three novels that received favorable reviews before turning to detective fiction. His first Nero Wolfe novel, *Fer-de-Lance*, appeared in 1934. It was followed by many others, among them, *Too Many Cooks, The Silent Speaker, If Death Ever Slept, The Doorbell Rang* and *Please Pass the Guilt*, which established Nero Wolfe as a leading character on a par with Erle Stanley Gardner's famous protagonist, Perry Mason. During World War II, Rex Stout waged a personal campaign against Nazism as chairman of the War Writers' Board, master of ceremonies of the radio program "Speaking of Liberty" and as a member of several national committees. After the war, he turned his attention to mobilizing public opinion against the wartime use of thermonuclear devices, was an active leader in the Authors' Guild and resumed writing his Nero Wolfe novels. All together, his Nero Wolfe novels have been translated into twenty-two languages and have sold more than forty-five million copies. Rex Stout died in 1975 at the age of eighty-eight. A month before his death, he published his forty-sixth Nero Wolfe novel, *A Family Affair*.

"The most important horror collection of the year."
—*Locus*

DARK FORCES

Edited by Kirby McCauley

(14801-x) $3.50

Including a complete new short novel by Stephen King

This new volume of 23 chillers contains new works by a star-studded roster of authors. You'll find spine-tingling tales from Davis Grubb, Ray Bradbury, Edward Gorey, Robert Aickman, Joe Haldeman, Dennis Etchison, Karl Edward Wagner, Lisa Tuttle, Ramsey Campbell, T.E.D. Klein, and many other masters of horror.

Get ready for terror as you encounter slug-like creatures who inhabit New York City's sewers, zombies who become all-night store clerks in California, a young boy who is kidnapped in his very own bed, and a multitude of horrifying beings and events.

Available in September wherever paperbacks are sold or directly from Bantam Books. Include $1.00 for postage and handling and send check to Bantam Books, Dept. DF, 414 East Golf Road, Des Plaines, Illinois 60016. Allow 4–6 weeks for delivery.

WHODUNIT?

Bantam did! By bringing you these masterful tales of murder, suspense and mystery!

NERO WOLFE

He's not much to look at and he'll never win the hundred yard dash but for sheer genius at unraveling the tangled skeins of crime he has no peer. His outlandish adventures make for some of the best mystery reading in paperback. He's the hero of these superb suspense stories.

BY REX STOUT

☐	13786	CHAMPAGNE FOR ONE	$1.95
☐	13548	CURTAINS FOR THREE	$1.95
☐	13651	IN THE BEST FAMILIES	$1.95
☐	14447	MIGHT AS WELL BE DEAD	$1.95
☐	13227	PRISONER'S BASE	$1.95
☐	14448	SECOND CONFESSION	$1.95
☐	13754	THREE DOORS TO DEATH	$1.95
☐	14449	THREE FOR THE CHAIR	$1.95
☐	13666	THREE MEN OUT	$1.95
☐	13145	TROUBLE IN TRIPLICATE	$1.95

Bantam Book Catalog

Here's your up-to-the-minute listing of over 1,400 titles by your favorite authors.

This illustrated, large format catalog gives a description of each title. For your convenience, it is divided into categories in fiction and non-fiction—gothics, science fiction, westerns, mysteries, cookbooks, mysticism and occult, biographies, history, family living, health, psychology, art.

So don't delay—take advantage of this special opportunity to increase your reading pleasure.

Just send us your name and address and 50¢ (to help defray postage and handling costs).